STRAGNO FALL
OM DOCTOR JEKYLL
ED POTI HYDE

STRAGNO FALL OM DOCTOR JEKYLL ED POTI HYDE

AB

ROBERT LOUIS STEVENSON

KIPS ED INTRODUCTION AB
MATHEW STAUNTON

SAMBAHSA TARJEM AB
OLIVIER SIMON

evertype
2017

Edihn ab/*Published by* Evertype, 73 Woodgrove, Portlaoise, R32 ENP6, Ireland. *www.ever-type.com.*

Presto titule/*Original title: Strange Case of Dr Jekyll and Mr Hyde.* Presto edition/*First edition* London: Longmans, Green & Co., 1886

Tarjem/*Translation* © 2017 Olivier Simon.
Tod edition/*This edition* © 2017 Michael Everson.
Kips ed introduction/*Illustrations and introduction* © 2014 Mathew Staunton.

Presto edition/*First edition* 2017.

Un catalogic notice tos buk est behandet bei British Library.
A catalogue record for this book is available from the British Library.

ISBN-10 1-78201-208-7
ISBN-13 978-1-78201-208-5

Schrifttehxen in Baskerville ed GREAT BROMWICH BOLD ab Michael Everson.
Typeset in Baskerville and GREAT BROMWICH BOLD by Michael Everson.

Covehr/*Cover:* Michael Everson.
Photographia/*Photograph* © Frances Fruit, dreamstime.com/ffranny_info

Druckt ab/*Printed by* LightningSource.

IKHTISSAR

INTRODUCTION

PAQUETS TROHFT IN UN VICTORIAN SEYF

Id 1886 novella *Strange Case of Dr Jekyll and Mr Hyde* ab Robert Louis Stevenson est, ye id sam rango quem ia *Metamorphoseon Libri XV* ab Ovid ed *Die Verwandlung* ab Kafka, oino iom staurst narns os physic transformation in literatures historia. Dayim redrucken, id hat inspiret pieces, Broadway musicals, ed pelu films, ed ia nams idsen eponym persons hant entret maung bahsas kay kyuses dissociative identitats-disaurdhen, wilda dumosweips, ed exteradet au impredic-tible sulouk. Elements tos storia hant bihto talga clischees in id landspect os popular culture quem tod ne est tem ops list quem idso successo suggestiet. Dank cinema, bragvyen versions, caricatures, graphic novellas, ed vasyalg references in alya media, tod est un storia quod fikerms ja gnohe aun hatta dehlge ghyane id buk.

Im nundiens leuds qui sa-leise id novella ye id prest ker en-falle onirs om stikelplen laboratoria, kwehpend potions, ed id lige uns hideus monster edghi sont surpris ab aunstehge od neter Jekyll ni Hyde est is protagoniste ios narn ab Ste-venson. Yaghi ies sont ies frequentst-ye udwekwnen persons bet id major part ios action est centret ep alyo, baygh minter maschour wir: iom prabh nesmeihnd advocat Gabriel John Utterson. Seimen Henry Jekyll ed eys alter ego Edward Hyde sont ies subjects tos stragnios fallios, Utterson de est qui endersoct id mysteir in quo est mukhtmel-ye oino iom aiwo kamyaptsten detectiven romans.

Tik ambhglanzes id texte revelet od Utterson est druve-ye is dohbro wiro pro tod job. Apart Hyde, is gnoht intim-ye vasyens principal persons. Richard Enfield, is prest weit-wodd qui descript Hydes crueltat, est ei nityis ed kerab. Sir Danvers Carew est oin em Uttersons prestigieusst clients ed behrt un brev adressen sieni advocat kun is biht maurdhen af Hyde. Bo Doctors Jekyll ed Lanyon sont ei sabikas ed hant ei betrust ir mohrtbrevs. Is est eti Jekylls advocat ed est bohn-den ab testamentar bereulens kay represente iom mysterieus Hyde sei is doctor mehriet we dispareihiet. Vasyi persons in in buk bayghe id samo netwehrg in quos kerdo trehvmos G. J. Utterson, kowpt-yos meticuleus-ye oral ed scriben scha-hidias.

In un storia pleno med suggestive-ye namt persons, Ga-briel John Utterson est un sibbeudend nam. Kad tod patro-nym siet mehmihes sem Britisch leisers iom advocat ed bukencollector Edward Vernon Utterson (1775 au 1776 / 1856), dehtormember ios selective Roxburghe Club pro bi-bliophils ed prominent ios diksmund ios XIXt secule. Hatta Anglicisants qui hant naiwo klun de tom real-mund rjienb-wuts proe-pehnde tod nam (utter-son) baygh ciautaung pro semquom qui collect ed niscript altern paroles (Englisch: *ut-terances*). In bo falls wey smos buden eysi rol os specialiste in ia sammeln ed analyse om documents, ed smos akster-ye en-couraget ad ses tem attentive face Stevensons texte quem Utterson est face ta ab Jekyll, Hyde ed Lanyon.

Gohd radh ar id texte os *Jekyll and Hyde* est dens ed com-plexe, anticipend ia lexical strategias modernisten scriptors kam James Joyce ed Vladimir Nabokov. In id tienjien En-glisch texte, id neud uns archayic, Alban ed ambigu voca-bular nilent id leisen, creet dwoi, ed dwinght al leiser kwehre kam Utterson skweitend un dikstexte kay ghabe ids merit.

Stevensons unique style est enevidencet ab id fact od id *Oxford English Dictionary* citet exempels ex *Jekyll and Hyde* ne minter quem 70s. Un kauwirtic proba ios werdkerdos ios autorios prehpt kun ghatmos Jekyll ye id prest ker ed kun id lige ios doctor est descript ka "sliv" (p. 35). In tod contexte (dwo veut prients tolkend nieb id vatra), to kwecto tik maynt od is est suaxurt. Dalger in id narn, lakin, Hydes arendatrice (p. 47) est descript ka habend *"un khiter lige, sliven af hypocrisis"* ed bihms it subtile-ye encouraget ad rekehnse nies prest pondos de Jekyll. Is behrt eti uno nam quod suggest un gver (Englisch *jackal* = "shagal") au nergven eiskwens (Englisch *to kill* = "nices"), ed eys inexplicable sibia con Hyde est un ayib eysi sonst-ye neigvos kleumen.

Id significance os Utterson prehpt in eysschi prenams. Is est meis quem un "werdentecton". Is est eti uno messager ed maghses hatta un prophet. Is est sammel Archangel Gabriel ed Iohannes is Baptiste, creet ed yist ab iom omniscient autor kay gnopihes quo wakyit in Jekylls practis. Dank ia mult biblic references in id novella est mukhtmel od Stevenson exspectit kem eys leisers esient kheissas dia ta nams. Esdi el leiser keungiet, is dikeiht Utterson quetro: khakus resiste id tentation os dughes un jinas ex id nam Hyde, is oiscript: *"If he be Mr Hyde,"* (…) *"I shall be Mr Seek"* = "Ismen Poti Tupes," (…) "ego de Poti Sok".[1]

Stevensons kaur de ia selection ed positionen os eys vocabular suggest is tant kieur dayir sien titule, valt-yod bihe perichohxt. Tod est un "stragno fall". Ka solg est id stragno jecto quod hat wakyen ad Henry Jekyll ed eys comorbaters, est id totalitat iom relevant facts, ed est id bayan tom facts redacto kay bihe chohxt ab un hoger instance, quo impliet od tod bayan est tem stragno quem ia wakyas id reconstruct. Kam ho ja diken *supra*, Stevensons advocat est suaqualifiet

---

1 Weidwos est id jinas un pichen different in id Sambahsa tarjem, yedschi tem bedebah : *"Hyde aptersokiem hatta do Hayd !"* is iey sib.

pro comsammel ia documents ed schahidias ed pro construge un coherent narn au, maghses, hatta un buk om pruvs. In tod regard, Utterson, swoproclamen experto pro vetatswassikas, est is prototype os Jonathan Harker, iom vetatieus advocat os Graf Dracula. Id ingenieus collage om brevs, journal entrats, phonographic transcriptions, ed reportages quod constituet Bram Stokers 1897 roman hat maung in commun con Stevensons texte. Quo lyehct in ia kowngbaykus inter ia diversa schahidias est likwn ei imagination al leiser ed id seductor force om bo buks residt in tod nescriben dord archetypen.

Id werd "fall" est eti darm-ye ankern in id mund os medicin ed est significant od penetrems id mysteir ambh iens eponym persons dank ia weitwoddias om dwo lieks anter quem per id intervention ios police. Uttersons prest reaction ant id stragno sulouk os Jekyll est suspece sem crime bet ye perodher id narn, ye meis bisweurght is an eys prient est sieug ed ia antwehrds eysims questions sessient medical (follia) anter quem legal (chantage).

In Englisch, *case* ne maynt tik "fall" (nomen) sontern yaschi plur gensa kwateln (diek, sack, wagin). Ye id sam weidos, vighabmos jaldi od *Jekyll and Hyde* est kam jects dohken do mutu. To est ver bo pro id scriben ios novella ed id finihto texte. Est suagnoht od Stevenson trohv sien initial inspiration pro id narn in un drehm.

> Ee-sisrehto mien kerso po quodgvonc intrigo; ed unte id dwot noct io drohm de id scene claus id fenster, ed un scene poskwo se dwifiss, in quod Hyde, apterdraht ob sem crime, sorpsit id pulver ed mutaformit in presence sienen aptersehkwers. (RLS, Januar 1888)

Ghehdmos, yinjier, skwites Hyde ka un genis archetypal balghbonem tyicen ab Stevensons inconscient. So archetype buit tun dohken do un allegoria sekwent id suggestion ias esor os Stevenson, Fanny. Ia nams iom persons pfehrste kyun potential allegoric skweiten eti Stevensons commentes de eys wi texte nos linkwnt neid dwoi. Tod allegoria buit poskwo etidohken do uno mysteir ed naiw explien ab iom autor. Id crehscend numer om speculations de quo wehst trans tod allegoria est uno meid os just kam meg kamyapt hat tod strategia obkwohken pro Stevenson. Ye id nivell ios texte, Utterson endersoct Jekyll ed Hyde sbei fall ed in id druna ios presentation sienen vrehmens kwaht is resolve id mysteir quod troublit iom: quis est Edward Hyde ed quod fangh hat is uper Henry Jekyll? Pro el leiser, lakin, id psychic taraghmen causet af Hyde est naiwo resolwt, ed quan id scriben schahidia os Jekyll endt ye id senst page ios narn, nies questions ed malaise continuent. Stevenson alludeiht Jekyll to ye id conclusion os eys "hol bayan ios re", quan is oiscript "quo vaht sehkwe concernt alyo quem mepet". Quo sehkwt est silence ed in tod silence dehlct el leiser nachehxe id material collect ab Stevensons advocat ed tekhnasse face el specter os Jekyll monstrueus id-on.

Kad nos meist formehnmos ep certain data qua Utterson ne hat aunkohldert. Quetro Edward Hyde quan is linkwt id practis os Jekyll? Hyde est id incarnation os quanto Jekyll sib refuset ka plaisures bet naiwo leitmos prosch dyehrce quo to maghiet ses. Jekyll ne kwaht narre ia atrocitats committen ab sien alter ego ed Utterson debses-ye ne dehlft tetro. Hams neid alyo cheus quem nudes nies imagination. Ismen advocat sib refuset id plaisure om oismauter pieces, drehnke vin ed wakhe sert. Kwe de Hyde perikwehlt theatres ed se fordrehnct? Id profundo cherkinia tos person ed id horror is inspiret altrims suggestent semject meg sombrer. Sont udwekwnt crime, extreme crueltat, ed torture. Id trahen ias lytil pieg ed id maurdh os Danvers Carew sont pruvs os aunlimite violence. Jekyll recogneiht ta facts. Quod tar ghehdiet ses meis khiter quem bate ed trahnes un mensc hin el nehct?

Tod question hat est exploret in meis quem 120 films, ops ye id detriment alyen aspects ios storia. Utterson biht daydey marginaliset we alnos myohrst kay dahe rewos ad superficial ster persons, romance ed sexe. Ia commercial-ye success-wentst awa films sehkwnt id itner ios 1887 piece ab Thomas Russell Sullivan in-yod un impatiento Jekyll hat sponden wehde Carews dugter ed mutawardht do Hyde kay sib ud-tehrge un gvaltic sexual relation con music-hall sehngverin Ivy Peterson.

Id 1931 film est un excellent exempel. Akapto pre id Hol-lywood censure code buit rigoreus-ye dostrigen, id linkwt neid ei imagination al smautrer ed Frederick March ieust-ye ielgv un Academy Award pro sien tamsil ka Jekyll ed Hyde. Eys alt social status oistambht ad Jekyll implehe eys pulsions. Is est impatiento de wehde sien fiancee ed brunges sem plen sexual relation menxu is sammel yehbhskwt Ivy Peterson. Pos sem waurmenincontren glect is tam sdue lent-ye in ays kamer, kunt iam passionat-ye ep ays crovat, ed tik id prematur intervention os eys collegh Dr Lanyon behrct iom ud etikwehre. In tod adaptation ios storia, Hyde est is "centeng" os Jekyll ed in tod forme udgvalt is sib un long-meiwrnt sexual relation con Ivy Peterson quod yed is naiwo consummsiet samt sien quantengnohn enokwo. Rouben Mamoulian ed eysi scenaristes Percy Heath ed Samuel Hof-fenstein kweiternt sem greiszones ios texte os Stevenson (Je-kylls kohlt wehnsa, Hydes aventures, ma Hyde attaquit Carew) bet sammel seinke id bfuxiongia ios storia dia id umum. Idmen film est schockant ob sien enscenen om sexual depravitat, violence ed Hydes repugnance—yed sexe criminals ed maurdhers sont commun in Hollywood films. Id de buk est schockant ye un profunder nivell ed nos dwinght dehlve nies khiterst paurs kay dadwe ad Hyde un lige ed un aptergrund.

Id leitmotiv ios fall peripleht kathalika id texte ye un literal nivell. Trehvmos practis eni practis, sgillen vulbhs eni sgillen vulbhs, ed id constant, neskapim presence ios seyf os Utterson. Tod maghiet ses ayt ka id surce os quanto maynt in tod texte—quantum aunstehgmos de id relation inter Jekyll ed Hyde est placet ed viemerct ex ia temost kantuns tos inanimat object. Id surce ios transformationsmagh os Jekyll samye est dohct eni plur gordsa. Kay ghehde recuper ia chemicals os Jekyll, Dr Lanyon dehlct entre id dom siens collegh, vrehnge id dwer do eys practis, ghyane un glasalmar ed extrage un liachic. Id gothic technique os dehke narns do alya narns est reproducen in id texte med id packbehnden om brevs eni paquets oisgillt ye meis quem oin stet. Lanyon yeist ad Utterson un brev wahid-ye ghyantu sei Jekyll mehrt we dispareiht. Id senst brev ab Jekyll est perisgillt samt un nov testament ed un hol bayan ios re sekwent iom. Ta-pet paquets sont guarden in Uttersons privat seyf, andamt in un kyal eni eys dom. Kay penetre ia mysteirs ios re de Jekyll ed Hyde sont lasim ghyane id seyf ed ia paquets ed interprete ia textes eni.

EN IOM BALGHBONEM

Nespekent sien popularitat, *Jekyll and Hyde* hat obkwohken ses un challenge pro illustrators ed, yinjier, ia kipwent editions sont meg rarer quem quo poittiemos exspecte. Yed to ne est un surprise. Ia detayls qua nos meist interessient ka leisers ed smautrers—ia apparence ed facts os Edward Hyde—sont frustrant-ye descript ab Stevenson ka indescriptible. Enfields rhayr-imkan os ambhrisses ia traits os Hyde— traits qua yed is sigwrt habe clar-ye in sieno ment—biht epidemic in id druna ios narn. Nimen ghehdt describe kam quod kwehct Hyde hatta starnd-ye seid ad iom. Quanto ghehdent sayge est kam bfuyowi kheissent quando glanzent kyom. Hyde est un balghbonem, un blank page ep-yod alter persons ed, poskwo, i leisers inscribe ir paurs. Quosmed tar tehrbiet sem illustrator bekipes tom mysterieus person?

In plur illustrations in tod edition ho chust risses Hyde ka un aunlige individu ed io invite el leiser ad fiker kam quod is kwehct. Ste leudher de dahe ei id kieplik morphologia in ia filmtamsils de iom, id lige uns horrible garguyl au, sei to satisfact vies fantasia, ia passionwenta traits os Klaus Kinsky. Ste sam-ye leudher de alnos fiker als. In alya kips ho tenten capture id intense aura os violence quod perambht Hyde depingend-ye iom kam un visual amalgame iom boxers ios inkapem ios dwogimt secule. Ter est neid dusformia. Hyde est biaur tik eni. Extos is est yun, muscleus, kreptic, swekwr. Eys agressionsimkan est tarkim ex eys okwi ed darmen anter quem ex quodkwe contranature arrangement eysen lige traits.

Alyo frustrant aspect ios novella est id absence os informa-tion dayir id "Incident claus id fenster". Id hol narn est construgen ambh tod moment, id epicentre ios psychic ta-raghmen causet af Hyde. Bet de quod tar leit to? Utterson ed Enfield vide semjecto terrifient in id lige os Jekyll kun so tolct ibs kata sien prestetage fenster ed bo vilinkwnt peri-schockt. Payn dwo pages long, tod est id cortst capitel in id buk yed woidam id mathmount semject ex id anun ios in-conscient os Stevenson. Quod tar kipo pro id? Id rissem uns wir claus un fenster (toghi est quantum is autor descript) leipst deception-ye capture id archetypal horror quod ema-net ex tod scene. Jekyll spehct nos kata sien practis, tolp quanten sombren desires is desperat-ye eiskwt probire ed en-derwaurge. Inkye tod rewos tyeict is ia experiments qua kyeuke Hyde; herschi nehce bo Jekyll ed Hyde unte id katu inter iens id-on ed superego ios doctor. Id fenster yinjier nos ananct un aziyatend glanez kya sombrest wangwls ios atmen os Jekyll ed to ho io piten bekipes.

—Mathew D. Staunton
Oxford, Mai 2014

DAYIR IOM AUTOR

Robert Louis Stevenson gnahsit in Edinburg, Alba, dien 13 November 1850. Ob sieno mal sieune parkwohr is frequent safers quawert contribuer pinwes eyso scriptor-talent yant un yun oumer. Eet 28at quan eys prest buk buit publien. In France ghiet is Fanny Osbourne, iam wohden mater em dwo purts ex ia Uniet Stats, ed enliubh-se de iam. Dwo yars serter divorcit ia ud sieno mann ed Stevenson gwohm do California kay gwive con iam. I ghiem in 1880. Stevenson bihsit maschour unte sien jumiung dank sien storias pro bo magvens ed balirhs. *Dr Jekyll and Mr Hyde*, publien in 1886, aungvihtihsit eys klewos. Alya suagnoht wehrgs os Stevenson sont *Kidnapped, Treasure Island, Catriona, Travels with a Donkey,* ed *The Master of Ballantrae.* Is mohr 44at in Samoa dien 3 December 1894.

STRAGNO FALL
OM DOCTOR JEKYLL
ED POTI HYDE

CAPITEL I

STORIA IOS DWER

Ustad Utterson is advocat eet un wir samt mukadar enokw, naiwo kwitern ab sem smeih; eetolct ye un srig, laconic ed embarassen weidos; protiedarnd sien senti-ments; yed so buland, maigher, decrepit ed yui wir plaisit ye sien weidos. Unte prienten samghats, ed quan id vin ei suasmohg, semject eminent-ye dabrono znieyc ex eyso spect: semjecto quod in druve naiwo gwohm do luce per wehkwos, bet quod expresseer ne tik ta silent symbols ios posdinner enokwios, sontern meis frequent-ye ed samt meis gwis ia acts os eys gwit. Austere nu dia seswo, eedrehnct gin quan is eet saul kay enderwaurge sien gusto dia lecker crues; ed quayque is kiem theatre, is ne eesestiup do oin pon dwogim yars. Men is hieb dia alters un periprobet tolerance; ed is yando stieun, quasi samt envie, de id desire intensitat involwt in ir agsa; ed is anter eetrendt vihehlpe quem reprobe. "Dientowo ant Cains heresie," ee-ayt is pedant-ye. "Sino mien swesgens lites kyom diabel ye ir wi weidos." Katha eet ops eys bayga ses is senst itirafim sabika ed is senst dohbros influence in ia gwits em nileitend menscens. Ed dia ti, tan i perikwohl eys logiss, is naiwo skieu sem skadh os change in sien swoweidos.

Aundwoi eet id kyudos facil ad Ustad Utterson; isghi eet bilkull indemonstrative, ed hatta eys prientias kwecto kihr ep un samliko catholicitat os suabuhsa. Est id gnohmen uns kienkiu wir dactum sieno nitia ja ghesorkmeht ab waurmen; ed tod eet id weidos tos advocat. Eys prients eent auter eysi samaserngs we qui is eegegnohsit meist diutos; eys amors, kam ghedip, crohsc meiwrnt-ye, ed nieudh ex i neid sonterkweitu. Hetos, aundwoi, id diemen quod yug iom ad Poti Richard Enfield, eys piern kerab, suagnohn wir urbi. Eet pro pleistens un enigma daume quod ex uter attraxit alter, we quod commun interesse hieb ies ghohdt aunstehge. Sekwent qui ghieng pri iens unte ir mingo promenades, bowert sieyg neid, kwohk aunsam-ye plic-tisset, ed prim samt visible rehmen sem kyantgwehmend prient. Nespekent to, ambo prihr bilkull ta dworisghangs, ies kohns ka bellst andem os cada hevd, ed kay brunges ta regular-ye ibs wakyit ne tik tyehgve alya plaisure waur-mens, sontern yaschi remane boder de besoynkal.

Unte oin tom kleiunias iens duxit hasard do uno smulk abwohndto strad uns orbaterweik os London. Anghen eekalt to un sakwno smulk strad, quayque id carricit wehrgdiens un intense trafic. Ids weikers, qui kwecto quanti sua-ielgv, emuleus-ye etiielgvskweer, ed deidikier med ornaments quo sib hiebeer udbeneficet; yoitkwe ia dukan-fronts, kam dwo roigs oismeihnden pehrnstern, stahr jasib-ye engwn tod aulice. Hatta mingos, menxu id kohlder sien andmantsto zinat ed remienit nisbatan kenkwehlen, tod strad contrastit bleigu-ye face sien tarn jawar, kam un piurn in un forest; ed med sien fresch-ye repicta stavens, sien suagarwiet glaughs, sien general kiestet ed sien vessel protiokwo, id attrieg ed charm fauran id spect al passant.

Ye dwo dwers dalger quem un wangwl, levi eusttro, id inghang uns aula interrup id ardehsa, ed terkye id sinister masse uns bina forstilb ids ghebel uper id strad. Oin etage hog, aunfenster, id skieu ne meis quem oin dwer ye id grundetage, ed ye id uber etage id blind fassade uns decrepit mur. Id jixay-ye anac ia symptomes os un sordid ed forloncto neglegence. Id chat idsios dwer, aun kinkino ni carkela, hieb dissquamen. Vagabonds ee-endergwehme in tod roup ed eeghneihnt kibrits protiev ids panells; magvi eewesneihnt ep id soyl; sem scolpwarn hiebit probiret sieno kniv ambh ia moldures; ed pon takriban oin generation, nimen eegegwohm ad chasse ti nekwayden gostens ni urpes ir sketha.

Poti Enfield ed is advocat eent ghangend ocolo id smulk strad; bet quan arriveer pri tod inghang, preter liv sien canna ed kyus tetro:

"Habte yu ja kaut tod dwer?" sprohg is; ed quan eys sokwi hieb yaht: "Est connecten in mien ment, nabahsit is, uni baygh aunsam storia."

"Druve-ye?" mlu Ustad Utterson, med uno mulayim-ye alteren voc. "Ed quodghi?"

"Ke vos narro," jawiebit Poti Enfield. "Circum tri saat uns deusk winter maurg, eem gwirlaynd ex sem stet ye alter bors ios mund, ed mien itner lit unte un deil ios urb quer mutlak tik fanars eent incontrable. Strads lit sekwos mutu, ed quanti swohp… Ta eent belucen kam pro un procession yed tem desert quem un kyrk… tem quem io vigwohm do un keyf quer anghen stets meis akowsiet ed bi-sehgnet ke sem police agent prehpt. Fauran io vis dwo gastalts, hetos un smulk wir qui klieup eustworts ye gohd kadam, ed cetos un maghses octat au decat bent qua drahsit ye hol gwis ex un skeirstrad. Kunghi arriveer ye id wangwl, bo stus protie

mutu, quo eet destull natural; bet dind wakyit id horriblest ject, ar is wir srigkerd-ye trah id corpos ias bent ed likwit iam ep id pavement, heulend. To tengiet neid lehctu, bet eet diabolic visu. Io hieb ant me neti un mensc, sontern ne woid sem balstohmt gigwahnaudh. Maidehsim, bidrahsim, siz id colnier tos fulan, ed brigh iom tsay prosch iam heulend bent quam ja periembh un smulk greg. Is perfect-ye gwup sien chienjwakow ed ne pit resiste, yed me glaz tem atroce-ye quem io me khiss lahn ab sem srig swoid. I reuschus leuds eent ipet parents ias magv; ed fauran prohp is liek quei ia habiet dolhc' bihe yist. Sekwent tom mertikwol, ia bent comwert hieb haben meis dekhschat quem gvol; ed tun habiet bihe kohnst id end tos incident. Bet id conduct ios liek ubfiell me. Is eet is classic routine practician, samt indeterminat oumer ed pinseing yed un akster Edinburg accent, ed takriban tem sentimental quem un gayta. Yed, isge ieg kam weysmee: ielgs kun is glaz mien prisoner, io vis id lige ios mertikwol craspe ed pallasce ob nicskwes. Io tierk eys menos, tem quem is tierk mieno, ed chunke leuds ne poitte bihe nicen katha, iegam bariem proscher. Declaram ei fulan od depens tik nos suwes med tod accident un tem mier scandal quem eys nam stehnkiet unte hol London. Sei is hieb prients au kleumen, esiemos besic kem is leusiet i. Ed menxu eems aziyatend iom med tavro, pelu eegigweupmos ians gwens apo iom, quas eent kam furieus harpias. Naiwo ho io vis un solg samghat om haineus faces. Medsu ians stahsit is fulan, se ornend med un buxianxu ed cakhinant chienjwakow; isschi biey, to io suavis, lakin is skieu dohbro enokwo, kam un druv demon. Is iey ad nos: "Sei yu beuwskwte capital ex tod accident, som okwivid-ye ye vies mercie. Cada swamen semper vanscht tik vergihes scandals. Pancte vies hissab." Weyghi

kup cent punds ud iom, pro i parents ias bent. Okwivid-
ye, iom tentit mutattitude, yed is suadyohrc od weysmee
ne iskwam lutf, ed is vicess. Is tohrb tun trehve denars; ed
mehnte ghi od is nos duxit tei stet querkye staht id dwer! Is
strieg sem cleich ex sien gep, entrit, ed gwohm tsay mox
con takriban dec pund oyra ed un cheque ios Coutts bank
pro id reste ed inscriben payghim al bertor samt sem nam
quod ne poitto udwekwne, quayque id est oin iom
chefpoints os mien storia; ed eet un honorable-ye gnoht ed
ops druck' nam. Id summ eet alt, yed id signature ghohld
pro meis quem tod, suppose id buit genuin. Emsim id lure
os kaue niesi fulan od to hol ghohd ses apocryph, ed od in
real gwit, anghen ne penetrit unte sem kellar dwer pre salge
tsay con alyanghens cheque ghehldend pro takriban cent
punds. Bet samt un alnos aunkyehm ed naydic ton, is mi
antwohrd: "Mae bayte, niem linkwsiem vos pre id bank
ghyaht ni pre ioswo encasseihsiem id cheque." Wey quanti
tun abgwahsam, is liek, is pater ias magv, nies fulan ed ego,
ed spens id reste ios noct in mien appartment; ed ye
aghyern, pos snidanus, comihsam do id bank. Ioswo anac
id cheque, ed sieyg io hieb cada raison os credihes id eet
fals. Noghi. Id cheque eet genuin."

"Tsk-tsk," iey Ustad Utterson samt desapprobant
enokwo."

"Io vis yu kheisste id sam quem ego," nabahsit Poti
Enfield. "Ya, to est un ghyalir storia. So fulan eet un type
con quom nimen deilskwiet, un druve-ye buxianxurjien,
eti un rjienbwuts, oin tim civs quiwert (quo kwehrt to meis
khiter) parkwehrnt id sell. Chantage, suppono, de un
honeste wir qui payght aun spehce ob sem yuwent agos.
Nun kalo id stet ios dwer "id Chantage Dom", schowi. Esdi

to, yu gnohte, est dalg ud explie hol," mlusit is, ed is forkhayiel-se samt ta senst werds.

Buit ghi Ustad Utterson qui protiebud iom sprehgend-ye: "Ed ne woid yu an is emissor ios cheque weict ter?"

"To kwehkiet mukhtmel ne?" jawieb Poti Enfield. "Yed ho vikaun eys adresse; is weict ana sem place."

"Ed yu naiwo sprohg de tod dwer?" iey Ustad Utterson.

"No, swamen; ho haben un scrupule. Mi est pelu kados iskwes werds, ob to me pior mehneiht de id Sensto Judcement. Ho id pondos od iskwes un werd est kam xubhes un petra. Yu seddte sakwn-ye atopp sem ghyor; ed id petra rollt, ed dreibht alya con se; est un prientlik geront (is senst anghen de quom yu habiete mohnen) quospet ghalv biht vihihn medsu eys bustan ed vies famila dehlct tun mutaname. No, swamen, id beuwo un reul pro me: ye stragner, tun ye minter ambisprehgo."

"Unghi baygh gohd reul," iey is advocat.

"Lakin ho chohxt id stet," nabahsit Poti Enfield. "Payn kwehc' kam un dom. Est neid alyo dwer, ed nimen gwaht ex ni in unte id ploisko iom fulan miens aventure. Sont tri fensters uperspehcend id aula pon id preter etage; neid uber; ia stavens sont semper cluden ed kiest. Ed est un camin quod deumt daydey; schowi nimen sollt gwive ter. Lakin to hol ne est yakin; iaghi binas tem clostern' protie mutu quem est kaurd sayge quer oin endt ed alyum inkapt."

Id couple naghieng unte un khvilo silent; dind: "Enfield, iey Ustad Utterson, "yu ieg prabh."

"Yaghi, mehno," jawieb Enfield.

"Yed etileikwt," is advocat etimlu, "oin poin' de quo sprehcskwo: Gnohskwo id nam tos wir quo volvih iam magv."

"Gohd," iey Enfield, "ne vido ma to harmiet. Eys nam eet Hyde."

"Hmm," iey Ustad Utterson. "Quod tar tengicit is?"

"Ne est facil descriptu. Eet semjec' skeir in eys apparence; semjec' diskhauris, druve-ye detestable. Ho naiwo viden sem wir quom ho tant deskamt, lakin payn woidim ma. Is sollit ses dusformen semquer, yaghi, yed khako sayge qualg mems. Quayque is kwohk rhayr-adic, lakin ne kwahm dahe sem precision. O Swamen, no, druve-ye, khako describe iom. Ed to ne est due mien memoria, ob est kamsei ghehdiem vide iom taiper…"

Ustad Utterson dar lyt oistioupyit okwivid-ye meg pensive. "Ste yu yakin so folossicit un cleich?" vi-suwiel is.

"Dorgv Swamen…" bi-sieyg Enfield, alnos surpris.

"Ya woidim," iey Utterson, "woidim mien question soll' kwehke vos bizarre. Seighi ne sprehgo vos de id nam alters person, est ob ja gnohm id. Credeihte me, voster storia hieb ja nac' mien hem. Sei yu habte est exact ep sem point, plais correcte id."

"Yu habiete dohlgen warne me," jawieb alter samt un touche os skude. "Zowngschie ho io esen pedant-ye exact, kam yu saygiete. So type hieb un cleich; eti is dar xeiht id. Ho vis iom nudes id, minter quem oin hevd prever."

Ustad Utterson kwohster deub-ye bet neti sieyg ject; buit is yuwen qui mlouyit. "En alyo lection quod lehrt mae sprehge," iey is. "Io aygve me fortolkus. Smad bides mutu maeti tolke de."

"Ex id budmen miens kerd," iey is advocat. "Smad mussafahe maeti, Richard."

CAPITEL II

SOK PO HYDE

Ye tod vesper gwirliey Ustad Utterson samt sombre brens do sien baclar dom ed sess ghom kay dinner aun appetitt. Mingos, quando tod dorkw eet khatem, is ee-seddt nieb id vatra, samt sem jasamat os turso theologia ep sien pult hin id clock ios jawaric kyrk swohn id midnoct saat, tun ee-eiht sober-ye ed khalal do crovat. Lakin ye tod noct, yant id skatert buit oistract, ghens is un kier ed gwahsit sien bureau. Ter ghyien is sien seyf, vien ex idso deubst part un document quod bohr ep sien vulbh id inscription os "Doctor Jekylls Testament" dind sess tsay samt un amiwawento chol pre studye ids mathmoun. Tod testament eet wiscript, ar Ustad Utterson, quayque is eet taiper maimour tosmed, hieb refusen hehlp ad redage id; ne tik stipulit id od, in fall os decess os Henry Jekyll, M.D., D.C.L., L.L.D., F.R.S., etc, eys quant possessions dohlg bihe bayght ab "eyso prient ed mukarime Edward Hyde", sontern inschi id fall os Doctor Jekylls "disparition au neexplien absence unte quodkwe prist uper tri calendar munts", saygen Edward Hyde fauran bihiet is waris os sayct Henry Jekyll ed esiet leudher ud quodkwe charge au obligation ploisko id payghen oiken smulken summs im members ios agor ios Doctor. Tod document eet diutos daumobject pro iom

17

advocat. Tod afflixit iom tem ka juriste quem ka partisan iom saun ed traditional gons os gwit, quei fantasia egaliesc ad nedebos. Tuntro hieb eys neweida de Poti Hyde isnahn eys indignation: taiptro, eet eys weida, per un brusk muta-wakyen. Eet ja destull mal quan id nam eet tik uno nam de quod is khiek etimanthes. Buit maler kun tod inkiep endue detestable kweitus; ed ex ia wandlik ed aunmathmouna mighels qua hieb tem diu misplaisen eyso spect, is advocat vis wardhe stayg un demon.

"Io hieb crediht to eet follia", is iey sib, sneigend-ye tsay id badbakht papier do id seyf, "bet nun bibaym an sia dusdecos."

Poskwo blahsit is sien kier sgwesen, enduit uno mier mantel ed trohcit kye Cavendish Square, tod citadell os medicin, quer eyso prient, is megil Dr. Lanyon, wik ed prim id menegh sienen patients. "Sei semanghen gnoht, tun siet Lanyon" mohn is.

Is solenno majordom recognihsit ed sellgwohm iom; aun dehlge intizare, is buit introducto do id mejeina quer Dr. Lanyon dorkwit mon con sien vin. Is eet un cordial, wal, opost, eroudho gentleman samt un prematur-ye albhascus kaysfitil, ed taragweidos ed gwaukana maniers. Kun is vis Ustad Utterson, is gwohl ex sien stul ed sellgwohm iom boghesor-ye. Tod affabilitat, quod eet in ia adets tos person, tengicit lyt actorlik; yed id tyohc ex druv sentiments. Boghi eent veut prients, prever dusti in scol ed college, mehnend sellst-ye de mutu, ed—quo ne semper wakyet bi quantens —quoy alnos plaiseer mutu in uters hamrahsa.

Pos sem fortolken, is advocat introduxit id subjecto quod tem desamat-ye beswurgh eys ment.

"Suppono, Lanyon," iey is, "od sollmos ses, yu ed ego, ies dwo veutst prients os Doctor Jekyll?"

"Meiliem ke toy prients habient esen yuner!" scherzit Dr. Lanyon. "Suppose lakin. Bet pau mi importet ob tem pau vido iom taiper."

"Kwe ne?" bahsit Utterson. "Io vos credih baygh bohndt ab commun paurskens."

"Prevst," buit id jawab. "Meis quem dec yars prever hat eno bihn pior excentric pro me. Is inkiep duswehrte, ment-ye, weidwos; ed makar som dar interessen ab iom in memoria ios prev kam leuds sayge, iblis pau ho io vis iom tuntos. Talg scientific nughs," nabahsit is doctor qui bihsit stayg kirmiz ob grassab, "habient esen kafi pro diswines Damon ed Pythias ud mutu."

Tod lytil dumoskaug brighit kam un balsem ad Ustad Utterson. "Hant tik chidt de un point os science", sohgn is; ed dat science (ploisko notaren ieus) ne passionit iom, is hatta namohn: "Sei est just to!". Dind, linkwus sieni prient oik secundes kay sakwniesc, iskw is id werd quod eet id ziel siens visite, sprehgend-ye: "Dil yu aiwo con oin eysen protegeits, fulan Hyde?"

"Hyde?" repetih Lanyon. "No, naiw aurn de iom. Ne in mien tid."

Ta buir quanta istikhbaras is advocat brigh hem do sieno mier deusko crovat quer is navolvit aun mukhlato tiel baygh sert in id noct. Tod buit payn un rahatnoct pro eys ment quod se forwohrg do mer temos, belaghern ab questions.

Id clocktor ios kyrk stahndios tem gadab-ye prokwem id hem os Ustad Utterson swohn six saat, ed so na-explorit id probleme. In-kap hieb tik tos intellectualo gono betact iom; bet taiper eet eysschi imagination occupen, wa suasaycter persclaven; ed menxu is eevivolvt in id opac temos om noct ed sien kamer samt clus cortins, Poti Enfields narn disvolvit wasaha-ye ant eys memoria. Is credih vide id immense

gafanaros unios nocturn urb; dind un person qui gressit jaldi; poskwo un bent qua curs ex un liekpractis, dind bo incontreer mutu, ed is mensco monster trah iam magv pre abdrahe aun ware aysa cries. Auti visit is in un sumptueus baytel un kamer quer eyso prient eet swehpend, drehmend ed smeihndo de sien onirs; et tun id dwer tos kamer ghyahsit, ia cortins ios crovat ablikeer gvalt-ye, is swehper sbud, ed ajaban! Is aunstohgit claus sien trem un ses qui periwieldh iom, eti ye tod saat kun quant rahiet ei eent zaruri stahe ub ed age kam is eet wohlen. Is person sub ta dwo aspects hantit unte id hol noct iom advocat; ed sei prist-ye so nierc, tun eevividt iom oisnehge samt meis nin do swehperdoms, we stehmbe stets meis oku, hatta ye vertigineuso syrat, bayna stets vaster gastradsa om fanarbelucen urbs, ed ye cada stradwangwl epterdrahe un bent ed linkwes iam ter hules. Ed dar ieu so person un lige quosmed is habiet ghohdt recognihes iom; hatta in eys drehms, is ieu sem lige, autah tod eet un dehlwrnt quod vanicit kun is oispohc id..; Yoitkwe gnahsit ed crohsc lyt ed lyt in id ment ios advocat un aunsam-ye akster, quasi chapachul curiositato de dyies ia traits os druv Poti Hyde. Ei habiet esen kafi, credihsit is, glanzes tom tik oins kay id mysteir kweiteriet, eti periswehndiet swod mysterieusa jects quando bihnt suachohxen. Is ghabiet tun id raison-d'être ios stragnios predilectionios siens prient, aulibt os eyso supodehsa, ne minter quem iom hayraneihnd clausen ios testament. Ye cada fall to esiet un vidwirtic lige; id lige uns wir quos inster eet steug dia tongjon; un lige quei eet kafi prehpe kay isnahe in id atmen os phlegmatic Enfield un khisses os dregh haines.

Pon tod dien, Ustad Utterson perikwohl assidu-ye prokwem id dwer stahnd in id piern smulk butiquenstrad. Aghyerns pre orbatsaats, vespers ender id citadmighel-

nuben mekhtab, ye wiswa beleucens ed wiswa saats os khalwa au menegh stahsit is advocat ep sienlibt wals.

"Hyde aptersokiem hatta do Hayd!" is iey sib.

Eys patience viielgv mizdo. Unte sem bell drossat crustenair noct, eent ia strads glat kam id plorpelp uns balkielken; ia fanars, qua neid annem flickerih, eewiwardhent inter luce ed skadh. Ye dec saat, quando ia butiques clus, id smulk strad bihsit baygh desert ed, speit Londons ambileudend stump rumor, baygh silent. Lytsta swons bihr aurim dalgtro: hembloska bihr kwahim ocolo id chossee; ed ir ghangstamps meg proswohbh im passants. Pon oik minutes Ustad Utterson eestahneut wakht, kun is kwahsit un proschgwehmend rhayr-adic legv stieup. In id druna sienen nocturnen reconnaissancen hieb is viswohdto diutos id bizarre effecto tyict ab id gress uns dar distant monghanger, kun id fauran vikwit ex id ambiblosk ed ia vocs ios urb. Yed eys attention hieb naiw est peridahto tem acut ed decisive-ye; ed samt un akster ed superstitieus prekhisses os heihvs sien ziel skulk is ye id entrat ios aula.

Ia stieups tus proscher jaldi, ed bihr strax dwis honarer kun inghiengeer do id strad. Is advocat, xyangend-ye, mox parmath con qualg individu is dil. Eet uno meg simple-ye dun desbuland wir, ed eys aspect, hatta dalgtos, isnahsit bei luurer un violent antipathia. Is ghieng seid kyid dwer, skeir id chossee kay gaines wakt, ed untitner traxit sem cleich ex sien gep kamsei is gwirlayiet.

Ustad Utterson sielg sien kulk ed kun alter stahsit pri iom, is tip eys oms. "Poti Hyde, presumpo?"

Sopet Hyde stiup retro, inannmend-ye id air nert-ye. Bet eys baysa ne durit; ed, aun lakin spehce seid kyom advocat, is ei antwohrd destull chienjwakow-ye: "Yaghi est mien nam. Quod eiskwte yu ud me?"

"Vido yu vahte stiupes in," jawieb is advocat. "Som un veut prient os Doctor Jekyll—som Ustad Utterson, os Gaunt Street—is sigwra vos hat tolc' de me; ed incontrend-ye vos tem waurmen-ye, ho credihn yu maghiete introduce me bei."

"Yu niete trehve Doctor Jekyll; is hat salgen," jawiebit Poti Hyde, blahnd-ye kyep sien gep. Dind brusk-ye, yed iter aun spehce ub, is nabahsit: "Quois gnohte yu me?"

"Preter vos prehcsiem," respons Ustad Utterson, "ke mi dahte un favor."

"Libter," antwohrd alter… "Quod tar?"

"Plais sinte me vide vies lige?" sprohg is advocat.

Poti Hyde kwecto kung; poskwo, kamsei is fauran bihiet gwaukan, is protiokwit ub chiaujaen-ye; ed bo stahr still unte oik secundes oistarnd ad mutus enokwo. "Taiptos siem recognihes vos," bahsit Ustad Utterson. "Kad to bihsiet util."

"Yaghi," jawiebit Poti Hyde, "valt od hams encontret mutu; aproposs, est gohd ke yu woid mien adresse." Ed is ei dahsit un adadh ed un stradnam in Soho.

"O Deiwes!" mohn Ustad Utterson, "kwe hat eischi enfallt id testament?" Yed is gwup sien reflexion eni se ed se grancit med danke pro tod unwan.

"Nunkye," bahsit alter, "antwehrdte mi: quois gnohte yu me?"

"Mi buit tolken de vos." buit id jawab.

"Quel tar tolkit?"

"Hams commun prients," antwohrd Ustad Utterson.

"Commun prients?" repetih Poti Hyde, med un rauk voc. "Citet ghi oin."

"Jekyll, mathalan," iey is advocat.

"Naiwo tolkit is vos de me!" scricit Poti Hyde in un grassa-badfall. "Naiwo habiem io credihn yu maghte lughes."

27

"Lutfan plais," bahsit Ustad Utterson, "yu vos forerghte."

Alter emiss baygh jahar un wild cakhin; ed unte oin instant, samt extraordinar okutat, is disandiem id dwer ed disprohp do id dom.

Is advocat preter stahsit still quer Poti Hyde hieb likwn iom, in megsto trouble. Dind bistohmb is ub id strad, haltend ye quasi cada stieup ed bringhend sien hand ad sien chol, kamsei un akster mentangst praeddiet iom. Id probleme is eet it perichehxend, sammel kun is eet ghangend, bieygh un quasi-insoluble categoria. Poti Hyde eet bleid ed skohrden, is tengicit ses suadighen aun visible malformation, is hieb un diskhauris smeih, hieb suloucto dia iom advocat samt un quasi-gver mix om timiditat ed deursia, ed is bahsit med un stump, strident ed pwolbrohgen voc; to holo plid adversus iom; yed tod hol gasammlos ne eet kafi pro explie id tuntro negnohn repugnance, id disgust ed id baysa samt qua Ustad Utterson dyi iom. "Sollt ses alyo ject, sib iey so gentleman, perplex. Est sigwra alyo ject, yed khako hihes id. Div mi indeulctu, soghi wir ne tengiet ses un civiliseit. Maghses troglodytic? Au to esiet id veut storia os Dr. Fell, au est id mer inikas uns cherkin atmen quod transwaurct per eys ghomenvulbh ed transfiguret iom? Todghi senst hypothese, credeihm... Ah! Orm veut Harry Jekyll, seinu aiwo ho skwit ep sem lige id signe os Satan, buit de ep tod vosters nov prient!"

Apter id wangwl ios smulk strad eet un quadrat place perambht ab aw ed bell doms, ye tod zaman pleista decheen ex iro prev splendor ed oistajern unte etages au appartments ab vasyalgens leuds quanten conditions: plangrehvers, architectens, bfushin verslynkwehrers ed directors om obscure entreprises. Oin dom, lakin, id dwot ab id wangwl, dar bieygh oin weiker; ed ant idso dwer, quod pors

29

uno megil pondos om opnos ed comfort, quayque ploisko id kehmberokwn eet mergen in temos, Ustad Utterson hielt ed kschongit. Un at khadim, in livree, gwohm ad ghyane.

"Est is doctor hemi, Poole?" sprohg is advocat.

"Gwahm vide; Ustad Utterson," antwohrd Poole, sammel kun is introduxit iom visitor do un plaut ed comfortable vestibule samt ghem tavan, pavet samt kakhels, chals (kam un rurdom) med id kweiter flamme uns ghyant vatra, ed meublet med precieus aigen bufetes. "Preferte yu intizare her nieb id ogwn, Ustad, we eiskwte yu ke dagho id luce in id mejeina?"

"Dank, intizaro her," jawieb is advocat. Ed is knigv olan-ye protiev id alt ogwnark. Tod vestibule, quer is mox mienit mon, eet un khauris vanitat os eys doctoro prient; ed ispet Utterson eetitolct de id ka id amatst kyal in hol London. Bet ye tod vesper, un kreus iendh eys mozg; Hydes lige hantit kados-ye eys mehmens; is oispruv (exteradet ject pro iom) satos ed disgusto de gwit; ed ex id budmen os eys mental depression, ia dansant inikas ios flamme ep ia glat bufetes ed ia bfuxionga mutaskadhens ex id tavan kwit guway. Is aygvit khisses rohmen kun Poole bad rik ei mehlde od Dr Jekyll hieb salgen.

"Saycte, Poole," is bahsit, "ho viden Poti Hyde entre unte id dwer ios prever dissection sall. Est to ver, kun Dr Jekyll est absent?"

"Kheptenn ver, Ustad Utterson," antwohrd is khadim, "Poti Hyde hat id cleich."

"Mi kwehct od vies mayster maung treust tom yuwen, Poole," nabahsit alter samt un pensive protiokwo.

"Yaghi, Ustad, maung," antwohrd Poole. "Buam quanti wohlen obedihes iom."

"Ne mehno od ho aiwo ghat Poti Hyde?" Utterson inter-rogit.

"Yallah, noghi, Ustad. Is naiwo dinnert her," jawieb is majordomo. "Ed hatta wey pau vidmos iom ye cid gon ios dom; entret ed salct opsst-ye unte id laboratorium."

"Gohd, vos vanscho nun un sell noct, Poole."

"Sell noct, Ustad Utterson."

Ed is advocat gwirliey, samt aghnuend kerd. "So orm Harry Jekyll," sohgn is, "baym ya is se hat snigen do naos! Is eet wild quan is eet yun; yaghi much diutos; bet Divs loy gnoht neid prescription. Sollt ses toghi, id kabus os sem veut synt, id cancer os sem perbohrgen disgrace: kwoin gwehmt, *pede claudo,* yars pos memoria hat myohrsen ed swoliubh exterxubhen id fault." Ed is advocat, dekhschat ab tod bren, eemimehnt de sien wi prev, obsokend vasya wangwls os sieno memoria, ibo kjiawxieng sem diablo uns veutios duspriebhe gwehliet do luce ter. Eys prev eet destull aunmambh; pauk mensci miegh lises id narn irs gwit samt minter apprehension; yed is khiss humilyet ab ia maung agsa is hieb kwohrt, ed wohs do un sober ed bayasen schakiria dayir ia pelus is hieb quasi commiss lakin gnebh vergiht. Ed reikend tun sien prever subject, is dyohrc un spehbliute. "So Poti Hyde, sei bihiet studyen," mohn is, "sollt arehge secrets, kyehrsen secrets wirtic de iom; secrets quibs comparen ia khiterst os orm Jekyll esient kam diewo. Jects ne dehlge natyehce katha. Me kreuseiht quando mehno de tom creature klehptend claus Henrys trem; orm Henry, quod un protiebeuden! Ed quod un danger, seighi so Hyde suspect id existence ios testament, is intizarsiet herite. Way, dehlgo age tik sei Jekyll sint me," nabahsit is, "tik sei Jekyll me sint." Iter oins visit is in ment, kam kladen in sien kers, ia stragna clauses ios testament.

CAPITEL III

DOCTOR JEKYLL EET DESTULL YOW

Dwo hevds hieb dohnen kun, kjiawxiengst-ye, is doctor dapihsit oin tom amaten dinners qua is eeswehdt ad penk au six sabikas, quantims intelligent ed mumtase wirs, ed quantims pritors om lecker vins. Ustad Utterson, qui eet oino iom gosten, udmien ceter nadimes. To eet khich-ye nov; proeghi tetyohc pelu dwogimtias. Quer Utterson bihsit prihn, is bihsit kamen. I mejbans gairn gwupeer bi se iom strehngo advocat, menxu i elangvers ed leudher-dingvi ja stahr ep id soyl; i libter etimien con tom discret sokwi, kay reswehde khalwa, ed sines ir ment relaxe, pos sem excessive vesseltsponda, samt id precieuso silence irs gost. Doctor Jekyll ne abvic ud tod prabhil; ed taiper kun is sess witerom id ogwn—habiete yu vis tom robust ed pletwost penkgimtiat, quos sliv lige anac, samt maghses quod khida, vasya kweitus om intelligence ed karam, tun habiete yu ghaben med tik eys attitude is oispruv dia Ustad Utterson un sincere ed warmo prientia.

"Wewienim wehkwe vos, Jekyll," bibahsit alyos. "Mehmte yu vies testament?"

Un proscher chehxer habiet ghohden kaue od tod topic eet kados; men is doctor id circumvenit vessel-ye. "Mien brave Utterson," iey is, "yu habte nassib con un talg client. Ho naiwo viden un wir tem kaurnd de mien testament quem vos; ploisko maghses tom haydic pedant Lanyon, de quo is kalt mien scientific heresies. Yaghi, is est weidwos un latif pwarn... Plais mae brovte... Un excellent pwarn, ed dar revidskwo iom; lakin is reman' zowngschie un haydic, ignorant, schekhiwent pedant. Ho naiw es' decepter ab quelkwe anghen quem ab Lanyon."

"Yu woid io naiwo samstohm de," nabahsit Utterson, se persteivend ep tod instable topic.

"Mien testament? Ya, sigwra, io woid," iey is doctor lyt brusk-ye. "Yu ja sieyg mi to."

"Vosge iter saygo," etimlusit is advocat. "Ho mathen semjec' de iom yun Hyde."

Doctor Jekylls paydrwnen face, pati lipps, palliesc, ed eys okwi dusk. Is declarit: "Ne eiskwo etiklues de. Kwecto dohbham neti tolke de tod topic."

"Quo ho matht est abominable," insistit Utterson.

"To khact change jec' de to. Yu ne ghapte mien situation," jawieb is doctor, samt sem incoherence. "Som in un muschkil situation, Utterson, ed exceptional, kheptenn exceptional. Est oin jec' quod wehkwos khact remides."

"Jekyll," nasprohg Utterson, "yu gnohte me: som semanghen yu maghte truses. Itirafte mi to ka rouna; spondo behrge vos ex id."

"Mien kyar Utterson," wohkwyit is doctor, "ste baygh maedwn, druve-ye maedwn, ed ne trehvo werds kay danke vos. Alnos vos treuso; confidiem bi vos anter quem ceteranghen, hatta quem bi meswo, sei mi etileikwiet id

37

cheus; bet credeihte me, to ne est quo yu fikert; ne est tem grave; ed kay lyt yowihes vies ment, vos saycsiem tod oin: quanlibt ghehdo io abdehe Poti Hyde ex me. Nun smad plais mussafahe mutu, ed mersie ed mersie... Ed kem addeihm just oin lytil werd, Utterson, quod som yakin yu siete suakwahe: tod est un privat re, ed vos prehgo ke linkwte id tyehce."

Utterson forsohgnit sien specto do id ogwn unte uno minute.

"Som bebeidmen yu perfect-ye acte prabh," visieyg is, sammel kun is oistahsit ub ex sien kursiy.

"Hayte," nabahsit is doctor, "chunke hams prichohxt tod topic, ed ye id sens' ker io spehm, en oin poin' quod skeulo vos comprehendihes. Soghi orm Hyde akster-ye me interesset. Io woid yu vis iom; is mi sieyg to; ed baym is hat beviden bowrley. Yed vos sigwro od ho un megil, baygh interesse dia tom yuwen; ed sei aiwo sleito, Utterson, eiskwo ke yu mi promitte imdadhe iom ed salvguarde eys interesses. Yu agiete it, sei yu woidiete hol; ed yu me rehmiete ex un gwaur vyige sei yu plais promittiete to mi."

"Magho vos garantie naiwo siem kame iom," protiem-lusit is advocat.

"Ne vos prehgo ke siete it," insistit Jekyll, ponend-ye sien hand ep alters brakh; "eiskwo tik maschrou ud vos; vos prehgo tik ke hehlpsiete iom in memoria os me, kun habsiem slit."

Utterson khiek enderwaurge un kwehster. "Estu," is bahsit, "to spondo ke siem."

CAPITEL IV

ID CAREW MAURDH

Takriban oino yar serter, in October 18—, London buit taraght ab un crime uns aunsam gvertat quod buit dar gnohter ob id hog position ios victim. Detayls eent pauk yed taraghant. Un bays weikend nedalg ud id Tems hieb gwahn crovat ubdrabs ye circum 11 saat. Nespekent id nebule quod swohbh uper id urb unte id maurg, id waurno remien kweiter unte id mierst part ios noct, ed glau beluc bleigu-ye id strad quod id fenster ias bays uperspohc. Sa, qua eet aundwoi in un romantic menos, sess ep sien sunduko quod lyohgit claus tod fenster, ed forkhayiel-se. Naiwo (kam ia sieyg, samt dakruflutts, kun ia narrit id scene), ya naiwo hieb ia tant khissto tem in pace con menscgenos, naiwo hieb ia meis crediht in id karam ios mund. Api, menxu ia sess ter, ia vis gwehme ex id bud ios strad un veut ed respectable albhkayso gentleman; ed kyant tom gwahsit alyo baygh desbulando gentleman, qui preter minter attraxit ays attention. Kun bo buir just kafi prokwem mutu pro wehkwe (quo tyohc just ender id fenster per quod ia bays oispohc), is veuter sellamiet alter samt uno nafassat politesse. Id subject tos wehkwen kwecto ne eet os megil importance; datghi is pfohrst, is tengicit tik

41

sprehge de un itner; tun mekhtab skieusit eys lige kun is bahsit, ed ia baysa gairn spohc id, idghi kwohk exhale un tem innocent ed udzamanen suamenos lutf, con lakin un certain legitim gurur. Dind ia mohgh sem spect ad alter, ed oistieun ob ia recognihsit in iom fulan Poti Hyde, qui hieb oins faungmoent ays mayster ed protie quom ia hieb khissen antipathia. Is dohrj in hand un gwaur canna, quod is eefifinghert; bet is khich-ye antwohrd, ed kwecto klu samt un dusarct impatience. Ed tun baygh fujatan un grassabad-fall udbrohg ex iom, ed is oistiempit med sien ped, swohng id canna ed suloukit (kam descripsit ia bays) kam un foll. Is veuto gentleman stiup retro, samt un druve-ye meg surpriden ed lyt offenden protiokwo; poskwo Poti Hyde bihsit effrenat ed wiegher iom ghom. Ed tun, samt kieplik furia, is vielk sien victim quom is sammel pliegel med un grandwn cutten, qua sprag honar-ye ia osta, pre id nayv volvit ep id chossee. Face tod horrible skau, ia bays bayaldissit.

Ye dwo saat gohr ia ed vien id police. Is maurdher hieb diutos abgwaht; bet ter lyohg eys victim medsu id strad, incredible-ye peristuden. Id gazd alat ios agos, quayque id eet ex un rar, meg dens ed compacto dreu, hieb dwibrohct sub id gvalt tos bawlawios rage; ed sem klor sbohrsten tetos hieb rollto tiel id nieber auluck—alter, aundwoi, eet nafanghen ab iom maurdher. Un beurs ed un gold saat buir trohft ep iom victim; bet neid genpian, ploisko un sgillen ed postmarken vulbh, quod shayad is eet behrnd ei postamt, ed ep quod eet script id unwan os Ustad Utterson.

Tod brev buit uperdahn ei advocat prue menxu is dar lyohg in crovat. Pos payn glanzus id ed kleuvs id narn ios wakya, is sieyg samt un solenn protiokwo: "Khako mayne esta habsiem vis id nayv; kad to est baygh serieus. Plais

ijapte mi id wak' kay mutavehso." Ed, aun linkwes sien grave wajkho, is hast-ye snidien ed buit ducen do id police station, quetro id cadaver hieb est intikalt. Payn-ye hieb is entren id cell kun is nuk.

"Yaghi, iom recogneihm. Ho id regret os vos manthihes od lyehct ter id nayv os Sir Danvers Carew."

"O Deiwes, Poti," scricit is commissar, "est to possible?" Ed fauran blig eys okwi ob professional ambition. Is nabahsit: "To vaht tyices maung rumor. Kad yu ghehdte hehlpe me ad retrehve iom vinovat." Is narrit bragv-ye quo ia gwenak hieb vis, ed pors id brohgen schtuk ios canna.

Kun id nam os Hyde buit swohrt, Ustad Utterson proe-akowsicit, bet kun is chohx id klor, is khiek etidwoie: makar alnos brohgen ed sbohrsten id eet, is recognihsit id ka ex id canna is hieb schohnct ad Henry Jekyll, yars prever.

Is oisprohg: "Est so Poti Hyde desbuland?"

"Is es' bo skaun-ye desbuland ed khiter, sekwent id wehkwos nuden ab iam gwenak," antwohrd is commissar.

Ustad Utterson reflex dind spohc ub: "Sei yu plais steighte con me do mien fiaker, duco-pet vos ad eys baytel."

Tunkye eet circum nev saat ios aghyern, ed id prest nebule ios saison. Un platu chocolatkarag spalv swohbh in id waurn, ed id windo dayim henslit ed enkasrit tod ganebos; menxu id fiaker snohg ex un strad do alyo, Ustad Utterson dyisit un daumost ardhem om nuances ed poigs os regwos; her id duskit kam ye end os epoin, ed ter luc un opulent brun, kam id bleigos os sem stragno conflagration; ed cer, unte uno moment, id nebule destull kwohk dissquame, ed un sliep strehl os diewo skiep warwntos inter ia swehrbend mighelsregs. Viso sub ta mimithav aspects, id trist weik Soho, samt sien meln strads, sien dusvehsend

passants, ed sien fanars qua ne hieb esto sgwest we qua hieb esto redaghta kay arke tod matam reiken os temos, tengicit, ye ia okwi ios advocat, kam launt ex un coschmar urb. Eys brens eent eti ios kyehrsenst khisab; ed quan is glazit sien woghsokwi conscicit is semquayt-ye tod terror samt quod loy ed ids dostrictors ghohd waurmen-ye impremes hatta i prabhstens.

Kun id fiaker wohgh pri id diken adresse, id nebule lyt swohnd ed skieusit ei uno murdaro strad, un gin tugur, un franceois makah, un schopo pehrnend trigrosch romans ed salats po dwo pennys, maung lumpvehsend magvens heudelnd in ia roups, ed maungens gwens maungen different nationalitats quas sielg, cleich in hand, kay pohe ir aghyernglas; ed iter nipohd id aumbernebule tetro ed perbohrg ud iom tod sinister atraf. Ed tod eet id hem os Henry Jekylls favorite, un wir qui eet hered uns quardel os million om sterling punds.

Un filface ed argwrntlikkays anua ghyien id dwer. Ia hieb un khiter lige, sliven af hypocrisis: bet ays maniers eent excellent. Yaghi, ia sieyg, tod eet Poti Hydes hem, bet is eet absent; is hieb riken baygh sert honoct bet abgwahn tsay minter quem oin horo prever; to eet nel-ye stragn, eys adets eent meg irregular, ed is ops ne eet ter; gheskye ia ne eevevis iom pon quasi dwo munts.

"Baygh gohd tun, vidskwmos eys appartments," iey is advocat; ed quan ia gwen bideclarit to eet impossible, "tehrbo sayge vos quis est so person," nabahsit is. "Is est Inspector Newcomen os Scotland Yard."

Ia gwen emsit un wajkh os odieuso joy. "Ah!" ieyit ia, "hat naos? Quod hat is kwohrn?"

Ustad Utterson ed is inspector glaz mutu. "Is ne tengiet ses baygh popular," observit senter. "Ed nun, Madame, sinte me ed Poti kem ambichehxmos."

Unte tod hol dom, quod ploisko ia parts ias anua remien sonst-ye tuich, Poti Hyde hieb tik occupet un pair kyalen; bet ta eent meublen samt luxe ed sell gust. Un almar pohld med vinbotels; id pliat eet ex argwrnt, ia skaterts elegant; un gohd pineg hiengit kata id mur, un hadia (quod Utterson suppos) ud Henry Jekyll, qui eet un druv connaisseur; ed ia kelims eent om plur tuges ed amat color. Ye tod moment, lakin, ia kyals bohr vasya kweitus od ia hieb est nuper ed hast-ye obsoct; povestis eent diaspohrt ep id podloga, samt extroslahn geps; andamliachics oistohlb ghyant; ed in id vatra lyohg un kowp os greis bur, kamsei maung papiers habient esen aydhen. Ex ta geuls exdohlv is inspector id stub uns glend chequenbukil, quod hieb resisten id action ios ogwn; alter part ios canna buit trohven apter id dwer; ed dat to confirmit eysa suspecens, is officier se declarit satisfacen. Un visite banki, quer plur tusents punden buir aunstohgen lyehgend in id credit ios maurdher, completit eys nraveihsa.

"Credeihte me, Poti," sigwrit is ad Ustad Utterson, siem kape iom. Is sollt leusus sien cap, sonst habiet is naiw apterlikwn tod canna, ni bilhassa destrugen tod chequen-bukil. Denars, vedim, maynt parwarisch. Nos tik sont zaruri intizare ke gwaht id bank, ed publie sokischitihars de iom."

To yed ne buit aun difficultats; paukghi leuds gnohr Poti Hyde: ispet mayster ias baysias hieb iom viden tik dwis; eys familia khiek bihe retrohft; is hieb naiwo bihn photo-graphen; ed i rar persons in stand os describe iom divers muhim-ye, swod commun observers. I samstohm tik de oin

point: id hantant sensation os aunwehkwos dusformitat quosmed is fugitive impress qui dyir iom.

CAPITEL V

INCIDENT IOS BREV

Eet fayront quan Ustad Utterson kwohr itner ad Doctor Jekylls dwer, quer is buit fauran introduct ab Poole, poskwo duct unte ia cucins ed un ghehrd quod hieb est un bustan, do un treb indifferent-ye gnoht ka id laboratorium au dissectionskyal. Is liek hieb kaupt id dom ud i hereds uns klut chirurg; ed dat eys wi gusta eent petis chemic quem anatomic, hieb changet id destination tos block ye id bud ios bustan. Eet id prest ker kun is advocat buit primen do tod part ios bina siens prient; ed is protiokwit id kayk aunfenster structure samt curiositat, ed ambiglazit samt un desamat sensation os stragnet kun is tohr id amphitheatre, prevst uperpleno med lasni studyents ed taiper lyehgend nogwod ed silent, ia tables klas med chemic apparats, id ploro straht med dieks ed packkalm, ed id luce pehdend muzlim-ye per id stikelcoupel. Ye alter bors, un gastieup lud kyun rudhsirdacto dwer; ed pos tod, Ustad Utterson buit viprimen do id practis ios doctor. Eet un plaut kyal moinihno med glasalmars, meublen, inter alya, med un enebspecule ed un orbatstable, ed uperspehcend id aula per tri duilic fensters samt isern stanghs. Ogwn ieydh in id vatra; un lampe eet daghen ep id pervase, ar

hatta in ia doms id nebule biswohbh teug ed ter, claus id chielde, sess Dr. Jekyll, tengiendo mortal-ye sieug. Is ne stahsit kyant sien visitor, sontern rexit un srig hand ed sellgwohm iom med un changen voc.

"Nunkye," iey Ustad Utterson, yant Poole hieb likwn iens, "habte yu klut ia novs?"

Is lieko krus. "Eent criend ia ep id place," iey is. "Ho aurn ia in mien mejeina."

"Oin werd," iey is advocat. "Carew eet mien client, edschi yu ste, ed gnohskwo quod mi est zaruri kwehre. Yu ne habte esen kafi foll pro kehle tom type?"

"Utterson, kassamo ant Div," plieng is liek, "kassamo ant Div od naiweti revidsiem iom. Spondo ep mien honor od hol est khatem inter me ed iom. Isghi ne eiskwt mien hehlp; yu ne gnohte iom kam ego gnohm iom; is est in salvtat, in plen salvtat; mehmte mien werds, naiwo siemos iter klues de iom."

Is advocat klu buxianxu-ye; is ne kiem ia febreus maniers os sien prient. "Yu kwehcte destull yakin de iom," iey is; "ed pro vies furkan, spehm yu saycte prabh. Sei gwehmiet do mahel, vies nam ghehdiet apparihes."

"Som destull yakin de iom," jawieb Jekyll; "ho yakinia sababs qua io khiek smyehrihes alyanghen. Yed est oin jec' de quod yu maghiete radhe mi. Ho… ho dact un brev, ed druve-ye ne woidim kweter dehlgiem dikes id ei police. Eiskwiem linkwes id inter vies ghesors, Utterson; yu judciete hakime-ye, som sure; ho maung trus' de vos."

"Bayte yu tod ghehdiet bringhes do repere iom?" sprohg is advocat.

"No," iey alter. "Ne magho sayge od kauro de quo bihsiet Hyde; hol est khatem inter nos. Io mohn de mien wi person, quom tod kadost besoyn hat petis expost."

Utterson reflex unte sem khvil; is eet surpris ab id egoisme os sien prient, ed sammel rohmt ab id. "Gohd," visieyg is, "sinte me vide id brev."

Id brev eet script med un bizarre aunstop khat ed signet "Edward Hyde": ed id mieyn, nisbatan bragv-ye, od is mukarime os ids autor, Dr. Jekyll, quei is tem aundecos kwih po tusent generositaten, ne tohrb swurghes de sien salvtat, somkwe habend wassic skapzariyas. Is advocat destull kiem tod brev; tod schohnk un seller color ep id intimitat is hieb soct; ed is miembh sib sems om sien prev suspecens.

"Habte yu id vulbh?" sprohg is.

"Ho aydht id," jawieb Jekyll, pre mehnus de quo id lit. "Bet id bohr neid postmark. Id hat esen uperdehn exterbaride."

"Poitto io gwupes id diulibt?" sprohg Utterson.

"Yaghi, yu siete meis suakehnse quem ego," buit id antwehrd. "Ho lust mien swotrust."

"Gohd, vidsiem," jawieb is advocat. "Ed nun oin meis werd: kwe buit Hyde qui hat dictet id giokien in vies testament in fall os disparition?"

Is doctor kwecto sa-bayaldissit; is periclusit sien stohm ed nuk.

"Io ieum to," iey Utterson. "Is mieurdhskwit vos. Nassib-ye yu habte nohsen."

"Ho daken meis bieda quem habiem tohrpt," jawieb solenn-ye is doctor. "To sessiet un lection pro me—Yallah, Utterson, quod un lection!" Ed is kohl sien lige apter sien hands unte uno moment.

Ye id udghang is advocat stopit ed lyt tolkit con Poole. "Aproposs," iey is, "un brev buit bright hetro hoyd: ka quod tengicit is messager?" Bet Poole antwohrd formell-ye

od neid hieb gwohmen ploisko baride-ye; "eti tik prospects," nabahsit is.

Tod malumat gwiwit ia paurs ios visitor. Id brev hieb gwohmt unte idpet dwer ios laboratorium; hatta biht script in idpet practis; ed in tod fall, hol dohlg bihe judcet als, ed dyit samt bikull tadbir. Pri iom, journalvenegs brieungh ir vocs pelu kikraghend ep ia trotuars: "Special edition. Schockanto maurdh unios Member ios Parlament!" To eet kam un vochet pro un prient ed client; ed is khiek ender-waurge sem apprehension ib un respectable nam bihiet dribhen do id srehtos ios scandal. Ei eet zaruri eme un delicate decision; ed makar is hieb maung jischin biadet, is biwohn radh ab alyem. Albatta, is ne beudiet ad to direct-ye, bet kad is prikapiet sem.

Lyt serter sess is ye oin gon siens wi vatra, menxu Poti Guest, eys premier scribe, wohs ye alter, ed ye id exact midvia inter bo ed ye un jamile-ye hissapto distance ud id ogwn, stahsit un botel uns particular veut vin quod hieb diu wict enderdien in id kellar os eys dom. Nebule dar swohbh ep id guraghto citad, quer ia fanars glimmereer kam carbuncules; ed trans id betaubhen ed pneigen tom fallt nebhs, id chepriene ios urb nawaurs unte ia magn aulices samt un swon lik tei os un staur wind. Yed ogwnluce udkwiter id kyal. In id botel se hieb id tuviere diutos dissolwt; id posyagorida purpwr hieb clarascen unte id wakt, kam per vitrals; ed id diew om warm osyern posmiddiens ep coteau vinghehrds kwecto intizier ke diaspohr ia mighels os London. Aun khisses is advocat slohmber. Eet neis wir quei is hieb kohlen minter secrets quem ad Poti Guest; ed is ne eet semper sure an is gwup tanta quem is mieyn. Guest hieb ops ducen besoyn bei doctor; is gnohsit Poole; is sollit sigwra woide od Poti Hyde

eet un familiar ios dom; is maghiet trage conclusions tetos: ne esiet tun sell, taiper, an is vidiet un brev quod exclariet tod mysteir? Eti, kwe Guest, qui connaissit khat, ne ayiet tod beuden natural ed obligant? Is scribe eet meg suaradh; is ne leisiet un tem stragno document aun skapihes sem remarke, un remarke quod deikiet id ieun ad Ustad Utterson.

"Tod re de Sir Danvers est druve-ye trauric," iey so.

"Yaghi, Ustad. To hat maung buden id public," jawieb Guest. "Is maurdher est weidwos foll."

"Eiskwiem aure vies mayn de tod," respons Utterson. "Ho un document her handscript ab iom; to remantu inter nos, ioghi payn gnohm quo kwehre med tod cherkin besoyn. Bet en id, id khat uns maurdher, est eni vies weida."

Ia okwi os Guest blig, ed is fauran sess ghom kay studye id passion-ye. "No, Ustad," iey is, "ne foll, yed un bizarre khat."

"Abghi un baygh bizarre autor," etimlusit is advocat.

Tun entrit is slougo con uno maktub.

"Est tod ud Dr. Jekyll, Ustad?" suwiel is scribe. "Ho crediht recognihes id khat. Neid privat, Ustad Utterson?"

"Tik un invitation pro dinner. Ma? Eiskwte yu vide id?"

"Ya, just un moment, dank Ustad;" ed is scribe pos bo papierschids nieb mutu ed assidu-ye comparit ir math-mouns. "Dank, Ustad," visieyg is, kun is dahsit ia tsay, "est un baygh interessant khat."

Buit un pause, unte quod Ustad Utterson namohn. "Ma habte yu comparen bo, Guest?" suwiel is fauran.

"Ustad," jawieb is scribe, "est un petis exteradet sam-kwehkia; bo khats sont samlik in maung points, just different-ye clihn."

"Destull skeir," iey Utterson.

"Kam yu saycte," respons Guest.

"Plais, naiwo bahte ad alyanghen de ta maktubs," iey is mayster.

"Niem," sieyg is scribe, "Comprehendo."

Ed yant is buit mon honoct, Ustad Utterson seyfbohnd id brev proaiwo. "Quod!" mohn is. "Henry Jekyll falsscript pro un maurdher!" Ed eyso sehrgo glohdj in eys veines.

CAPITEL VI

REMARKABLE INCIDENT OS DOCTOR LANYON

Wakto dohn; tusents punden buir ambhanacen ka mizdo, idghi nehc os Sir Danvers eet kwaht ka un public injustice; bet Poti Hyde hieb disparihn ex id gnohsa ios police kamsei is habiet naiw existen. Maung ex eys prev buit exdighomt, edghi hol eet duskleumen: narns gwohm do luce de id crueltat ios wir, sammel tem rhayr-kheissas ed tem violent, de eys vil gwit, ed eys stragnens sokwis, de id haines quod hieb kwecto perambht eys carriere; bet quer is taiper wohs, neid kwehster. Pon is hieb likwn id dom os Soho ye id aghyern ios maurdh eet kamsei is habiet abstumt; ed tadrijan, in id druna ios wakt, Ustad Utterson inkiep ganises ex id wierme sienen emotions, ed retrohv sakwnia. Id nehc os Sir Danvers eet, sekwent eys menos, un pior gwaur kwoina po id disparition os Poti Hyde. Taiper kun tod khiter influence hieb abswohnden, un nov gwit inkiepit pro Dr. Jekyll. Is sielg sien khalwa, udnovit sien relations con sien prients, rebihsit ir familiar mejban ed entreteiner; ed menxu is hieb esto semper gnoht pro charitat, is kwit ne minter pro religion. Is eet besic, gwahsit meis dworis, is lit wal; eys lige kwohkit ghyahe ed kwitres,

kam per un introspective insaf; ed unte meis quem dwo munts, is doctor buit in pace.

Dien 8 Januar Utterson hieb dinnern bei doctor con uno smulk hamrahsa; Lanyon eet ter; ed id lige ios mejbanios mutaspohc ex oin do alter kam unte ia veuta diens quan eent un trio inseparablen prients. Dien 12, ed iter dien 14, is advocat trohv cluden dwer. "Is doctor est confinet hemi," Poole sieyg, "ed vidt nimen." Dien 15, is iter pit, ed iter ne buit admitten; ed seswehdus taiper pon ia dwo akhir munts vide sien prient quasi cadadien, is pohnd tod reiken os khalwa kardu tehltu. Ye id penkt epoin is dorkwit con Guest; ed ye id sixt is gwahsit bi Doctor Lanyon.

Tetro buit is bariem admiss; bet quan is gwohm in, is buit schocken ab id change tyohct in id apparence ios doctor. So kwohk behre sien decess-ischtiharo scriben ep sien lige. So eroudh wir hiebit bihn pall ed lagar; is eet okwivid-ye kalver ed veuter; yed ne tant-ye ta znaycs os oku physic degveihsa attraxeer id attention ios advocat quem id profundo terror diutis is credih dyehrce in eys ok ed ment. Quayque neshayad biey is doctor id mohrt, yed to buit quod Utterson buit tenten ab suspece. "Ya," mohn is; "is est liek, is sollt gnohe sien wi afiya ed od eys ajal vaht gwehme; ed woide to est meis quem is ghehdt tehle." Lakin quan Utterson sieyg un remarke de eys newal protiokwo, buit samt megil taschabyth od Lanyon se declarit mehrtur.

"Ho haben un schock," iey is, "ed naiwo siem ganises. Est un questiom om hevds. Gohd, gwit buit khauris; ho kamt id; yaghi Ustad, eekamo id. Yando mi saygo od sei gnohiems quant, esiemos masrourer de slites."

"Jekyll est ischi sieug," observit Utterson. "Habte yu viden iom?"

Bet id wajkh os Lanyon changit, ed is liv un tremblant hand. "Vanscho neti vide Dr. Jekyll ni klues de iom," iey is med un jahar yed aygswehner voc. "Basta de tom person; ed vos prehgo ke mi behrcte ud cada allusion ad semanghen quom ayo mortu."

"Tsk-tsk," iey Ustad Utterson; dind pos un forlonct pause, "Ne magho io kwehre semject?" suwiel is. Smos tri baygh veut prients, Lanyon; ne vahms kafi etigwive pro bepriente alyens."

"Neid ghehdt ses kwohrn," jawieb Lanyon; "sprehcte yuswo."

"Is ne volt vide me," iey is advocat.

"To ne me surprindt," buit id response ios doctor. "Sem dien, Utterson, quando habsiem mohrt, kad yu gwehmsiete do manthes id contexte os to. Ne poitto sayge vos. Entrim, sei yu maghte na-sedde ed mi tolke de alya jects, bihakkillah, tun plais mante; bet sei yu khacte abdehe tod balstohmen topic, tun bismillah abgwahte, ioghi neti ghehdo tehle to."

Yant is hieb gwirlayn, Utterson sess ghom ed scripsit ad Jekyll, schikayndo de sien exclusion ex eys hem, ed sprehgend de id cause tos biedan brehgo con Lanyon; ed posdini ei ghohd un long antwehrd, ops samt un baygh pathetic werden, ed yando sombre-ye mysterieus. Id cheid con Lanyon eet incurable. "Io ne blame nies veut prient," scripsit Jekyll, "yed smyehro eys mayn ke tehrbmos naiwiter ghate. Nuntos acskwo un gwit os extreme khalwa; mae ste surpriden, ed mae bedwoite, sei cludo ops mien dwer hatta ad vos. Plais comprehendte ke kwehro mien wi sombre itner. Mi ho infligen un kwoina ed un danger qua khako name. Ka magno synter sessiem isschi magno paytter. Naiwo habiem io mohnen tod ardh ghehdiet

69

arehge un tem schawngdaneihnd place pro payttens ed terrors; yu Utterson ghehdte kwehre oin ject kay legverihes tod fat, ed tod ject est respecte mien silence." Utterson stieun; id sombre influence os Hyde hieb abswohndt, is doctor hieb rict sien veut activitats ed prientias; oin hevd prever spons id prospect uns vessel ed honorable geros; ed taiper, unte uno moment, prientia, mentpace ed id hol khanliawng os eys gwit hieb kwohlpen. Un tem mier ed precipiten change pfohrst kye follia; bet yeji ia maniers ed werds os Lanyon, ter sollit ses un profunder sabab.

Oin hevd serter, Dr. Lanyon lyohgit in crovat ed naiwo restahsit tetos hin is mohr pos penkdem diens. Ye id noct pos id daunos, quer is hieb maung traurn, Utterson andiem id dwer siens bureau, ed, seddend ter sub id melankholic luce uns kier, vien dind pos ant se un vulbh uperdehn exterbaride-ye ed pechaten med id sgill os eys mortu prient. "PRIVAT: WAHID-YE pro G.J. Utterson, ed *destructu nelisen* in fall os eys predecess," eet scriben baygh vidil-ye; ed is advocat redwoyit dyies tos mathmoun. "Ho lust oin prient hoyd," mohn is, "vahm io luses alyo nun?" Is vimakhkoumih tod baysa ka desloyal, ed brohg id sgill. Eni eet alyo vulbh, kathalika pechaten ed uperscriben med: "mae ghyane pre id mohrt au disparition os Dr. Henry Jekyll." Utterson khiek truses sien okwi. Yaghi, eet disparition; iter her wohs nieb mutu ia werds disparition ed Henry Jekyll, her iter tem quem in id absurdo testament quod is hieb diutos redaht idsi autor. Bet in id testament, tod enfall gwohm ex id buxianxu inspiration os Poti Hyde; id eet tik nuden po un pior clar ed abominable maxam. Handscriben ab Lanyon, quod ghehdt id mayne? Uno mier curiositat lahsit iom palek, kem infrangiet id prohibition ed sammel mergiet do id budmen tom mysteirs; bet

professional honor ed id trust os eys mortu prient uper-wohnd; ed id paquet vikih do id deubst os eyso seyf.

Est oin ject arke sien curiositat, bet alyum est dehme id; ed ab tod dien est dwoyim an Utterson desirit id hamrahsa os sien survivend prient samt id sam las. Is dar mohn lutf-ye de iom; bet eys brens eent beghspace ed bayasen. Is yed gwahsit eys hem; lakin kad is eet rohmen ab ne bihe sisen gwehme in ed, in sien kerd, preferit bahe con Poole ep id soyl ed perambht ab ia air ed swons ios dworis citad quem admiss do id dom os voluntar kyalbehnden, ed sedde ed bahe con ids negwahet zahid. Poole hieb eti yik destull-ye ghyalir novs ad permehlde. Iswert liek stets meis confinit-se in id practis uper id laboratorium, quer is hatta swohp yando; is eet yui ed ajiz, bihsit stets-ye taciturner, ed neti lis; is kwohk praedden ab sweurgh. Utterson tem viswohd id samia tom reports quem is stets minter faungmoenit.

CAPITEL VII

INCIDENT CLAUS ID FENSTER

Wakyit ye Mingo, quan Ustad Utterson kwohr sien adic ghango con Poti Enfield, od ir itner iter lit unte id niebstrad; ed kun ies gwohm ant id dwer, bo stopeer kay dyies id.

"Badghi," iey Enfield, "tod storia est khatem. Naiweti revidsiemos Poti Hyde."

"Spehm no," sieyg Utterson. "Vos ho io aiwo bahn od ho vis iom oins, ed khisst kam yu repulsion?"

"Eet impossible kwehre oiter aun khisses alter," jawieb Enfield. "Aproposs yu sollte ayus me un asel ob ne recogneihvs tod eet un caudgatva kye Dr Jekylls hem! Est part-ye bi-sabab vos sei ho aunstohgen to sekwos."

"Tun yu bad trohv?" nabahsit Utterson. "In tod fall, neid nos stambht entre id aula ed glanzes kya fensters. Kay sayge ver, ne som rassuret de tom orm Jekyll; ed hatta extos, kheisso od id presence uns prien' maghiet ei ses sislew."

Id aula eet baygh khuld ed lyt loim, ed pleno med precoce regwos, quayque in id waurn, hog uper, dar blig eurehpdiewo. Id medyum iom tri fenstern eet pwolghyant; ed seddend indom claus id, annmend id dworis air samt

un aunfin-ye yui wajkho, kam semo mayuss prisoner, Utterson vis Dr Jekyll.

"Hey, Jekyll!" is cricit. "Ke yu leitte waler!"

"Leito baygh ghem, Utterson," jawieb is doctor skeud-ye, baygh ghem. "Niem etigwive diu, al-hamdulillah!"

"Yu pior mante dombohndt," iey is advocat. "Yu waniete ses dworis, kwehleihnd vies sehrg kam Poti Enfield ed ego. (En mien cousin—Poti Enfield—Dr Jekyll.) Gwehmte ghi; kufyet vies hat ed lyt sayrante con nos!"

"Ste baygh sell," kwohster alter. "Kamiem baygh; bet no, no, no, to est druve-ye impossible; ne deurso. Betghi, Utterson, som meg masrour de vide vos; to est un baygh megil plaisure; gairn habiem prohgen vos ed Poti Enfield ke gwehmte ub, bet mien kyals sont chapachul."

"Tunghi," iey is advocat suamenos, "id sellst ghehdmos kwehre est mane her ghom ed vos bahe ex quer stahms."

"Est just quo sa-venturim ad propones," respons is doctor smeihnd. Yed ta werds buir kaurd-ye swohrn, pre id smeih buit abwaurgen ex eys lige ed succedden ab un wajkh uns tem abjectios terror ed desperation, quem id glohdj idpet sehrg iom dwo gentlemans niter. Ghohdeer tik dyehrce id, idghi fenster buit fujatan slahn clus; bet tik dyehrce hieb est kafi, ed ies abvols ed likw id aula aunwerd. Inschi silence, ies tohr id niebstrad; ed ne pre ies hieb nact un jawarperigumt, quer hatta ye uno mingo eet dar sem chepriene, vivols Poti Utterson ed spohc sien sokwi. Bo eent pall; ed ir okwi inikies id sam dekhschat.

"Div indeulctu nos, Div indeulctu nos," repetihsit Ustad Utterson.

Bet Poti Enfield tik nuk grave-ye ed kwohryit sien silent ghang.

CAPITEL VIII

ID SENSTO NOCT

Sem vesper pos dinner, Ustad Utterson eet seddend prokwem sien vatra, kun is buit surpris ab bihe faungmoenen ab Poole.

"Yallah, Poole, quod bringht vos hetro?" sieyg is honarye; ed iter spehcend iom, "Quod wakyet vos? Est is Doctor sieug?"

"Ustad Utterson," iey is wir, "semjec' leit skeir!"

"Plais seddte ghom, ed en un glas vin pro vos, sieyg is advocat. Nun mae spehdte, ed gjuchiente mi quo yu eiskwte.

"Ustad," jawiebit Poole, "yu woid is doctor hat viswohdt se kyalbehnde. Is tun se hat iter kyalbohndt in id practis; ed to ne kamo, Ustad—ke mehro sei kamo to. Ustad Utterson, vos sigwro, ho paur!"

"Vedim, mien brave," iey is advocat, "tolcte mi. Quod daht vos paur?"

"Pon takriban oin hevd ho io paur," respons Poole, "ne antwehrdend eysi question; ed neti ghehdo tehle to."

Id firasat ios khadim confirmit plaut-ye eys wehkwos; is neti hieb darmen; ed ploisko id moment kun is hieb prest itiraft sien paur, is hieb naiwo spohcto do ia okwi ios

advocat. Tunkye remien is seddend, id nedrohncto glas vin post ep sien genu, ed oistarnd uni pelpkantun. "Neti tehlskwo to," repetihsit is.

"Hayte Poole," iey is advocat, "vido yu habte sem dohbro raison; vido od es' druve-ye semjec' quod ne leit skeir. Plais peitte narre mi quo to est."

"Mehno hat wakyen semject faul," sieyg Poole, braungh-ye.

"Faul?" exclamit is advocat, destull dekhschat, ed quasi parat ad pighres de to. "Quod est faul? Quod maynte yu?"

"Ne deurso sayge, Ustad," nabahsit alter; "bet maghiete yu gwehme con me kay yuswo vighapte?"

Ka saul antwehrd, Ustad Utterson stahsit ub ed enduit hat ed gaban; yed is meg stieun kun is vid kam maung rohmen buit id wajkho ios majordomios, ed kad is kathalika stieun de vide id nedrohnct vin in id glas ios ambikwol, kun so repos id pre abgwahe.

Eet un wild, srig, saisonwirtic noct os Mart, samt un pall hilal, quod tengicit supihn ab id wind, ed luc apter un diaphen ed legv texture ex feuctil disfibern nebhs. Id windo muschkilih tolke, ed erudh liges kam med un bich. Id kwohk eti abfirsche passants ex ia strads, meis quem biadet; ed Ustad Utterson mohn ya is hieb naiwo vis tod part os London tem desert. Isghi viensch id contrar; isghi hieb naiwo tem vanschto dehlge se sehnde olan-ye bayna sien congeners; ed makar cys ment alexit ud to, tod khiek arke un schteurmend anticipation os calamitat. Id place, quan arriveer tetro, pohld med tik wind ed duil, ed ia teun drus in id bustan vrohsch mutu engwn id sayp. Poole, qui hiebit proghanct unte id hol itner ye oin au dwo stieups perodh, taiper stopit fauran medsu id trotuar, ed speit id preusend weter, sduit sien hat ed swohmbh sien chol med un rudho

gep-handchirk. Nespekent id spehdo tos gumt, ne eet swoido due id marche quod is tiers, sontern tod uns angstios quod iom strangulit, eysghi face eet bleid ed eys voc, kun is bitolkit, braungh ed brohct.

"Gohd, Ustad," iey is, "hams arrivet, ed Div mehghtu mae khitert tyohc."

"Amen, Poole," sieyg is advocat.

Poskwo is khadim stus destull discret-ye; id dwer ghyahsit, protiedarn ab id zangir; ed entos un voc suwiel: "Ste yu, Poole?"

"Hol leit wal," antwohrd Poole. "Ghyante."

Id vestibule, quetro penetreer, eet bleigu-ye beluct; uno mier ogwn hieb esto daght, ed claus id vatra wohs id hol personel, ner ed ster, comkowpen kam un owenchurd. Kun ia vis Ustad Utterson, ia bays buit lambht ab nerveusa steuns; ed ia cokwin, scriend: "Al-hamdulillah! Her gwehmt Ustad Utterson!" se elien kyom kam kay glabe iom.

"Quod tar? Quod tar? Quod kwehrte yu quants her?" suwiel sour-ye is advocat. "Est baygh irregular, baygh incorrect; sei is woidiet, vies mayster nel-ye esiet satisfact."

"Ob quanti baynt," iey Poole.

Nimen protestit, ed buit uno mier silence; eet aurn tik ia bays, qua hiebit biplangen baygh honar-ye.

"Taycte!" iey ay Poole, med un furieus ton quod bevis eys personal erghen. (Obghi, quando ia bays hieb stayg auct id yoinkjiae siens riouda, quanti hieb trohst ed vols kyid inner dwer samt baysa ed anxietat.) "Ed nun, wohkwyit is majordom ei cucinpwarn, "dahte mi un schamdan, ed vahms panges to." Ed tun is prohg Ustad Utterson ke sohkwit iom, ed iom duxit do id bustan.

"Taiper, Ustad," is ei sieyg, "yu siete age bilkull minst honar. Eiskwo ke yu aurte bet ne ke yu bihte aurn. Ed bilhassa, Ustad, sei aiwo is prehgiet vos ke entret, mae gwahte in!"

Ob tod imprevis conclusion, Ustad Utterson hieb uno nerveuso spreud quod quasi distulit iom; yed is mudh ub ed sohkwit iom majordomo do id laboratorium treb, dind per id dissection amphitheatre, empediset med schischees ed flaskens, bad arrivit pod id drab. Ter, Poole znieyc ei kem is retrostiupit bigon ed ieur; ed isswo, ponus ghom id schamdan ed okwivid-ye sammelvs sien hol gwaukania, stigh up ia stieupens ed med un dusdarm hando stus id serge ios practisdwer.

"Doctor, Ustad Utterson prehct ke poitte entre," mohld is. Ed sammel motionit is dastur-ye ei advocat kem akowsicit.

Un schaki voc antwohrd entos: "Saycte ei od mi est impossible primes quelkwe."

"Gohd, Doctor," iey Poole, samt in sien voco kam un triumph accent. Dind, reghendus id schamdan, is nih tsay Ustad Utterson unte id aula do id magno cucino, quer id ogwn eet sgwest ed quer targans gvohmb ep ia flises.

"Ustad," iey is, spehcend do eys okwi, "Kwe tod eet id voc miens mayster?"

"Id swohn baygh changevs," jawieb is advocat, "baygh pall," yed protietehlend id spect ios majordomo.

"Changevs? Toschi mayno!" iey is khadim. "Som pon dwogim yars in id dom tos wir, kamtar ghehdiem io rhalte de eys voc? No, Ustad, mien mayster hat disparihn oct diens prever, quando hams aurn iom crie id nam os Div; ed *quis* est ter instet iom, ed *ma* so wehst ter, Ustad Utterson, est semject quod kyeuct id Warwn!"

"Tod est un baygh stragno storia, Poole, hatta un foll storia, mien prient," iey Ustad Utterson, dehnkend sien fingher. "Suppose quant est kam yu supponte, suppose Dr Jekyll buit—ya—maurdhen, quod tar duciet iom maurdher ad mane? To ne est logic, ne kemall."

"Gohd, Ustad Utterson, ste un wir kaurd convinctu, yed vahm pites," iey Poole. "Unte tod hol akhir hevd (yu dehlcte gnohe), isge, au el, au quelkwe gwivt in tod practis, hat crien nocts ed diens po sem sorte os pharmac aun pehnde oin quod iom dohbh. Is semquando—tolko ya de mien mayster—scripsit sien wehlens ep un genpian is xubh do id nardban. Ne hams hab' neid alyo unte ta oct akhir diens; tik genpians ed cluden dwer; ed hatta ia chifans wey likwam pod tod dwer, ed qua is brigh intro rahas-ye kun nimen vis iom. Yaghi Ustad, cadadien, ed hatta dwis au tris cadadien, eent tik wehlens ed keupens, ed ho tohrben drahe bi vasyens samsarapothekers ios citad. Ielgs kun io brigh tsay id product, eet un nov genpian kay mi sayge yises id tsay ob id ne eet pur, ed un nov wehlen pro alyo venkel. Tod product, Ustad, ifrat wanmos, pro quod neud io ne woid."

"Habte yu gwupen oin tom genpians?" sprohg Ustad Utterson.

Poole obsokit sien gep ed salgih tetos un alnos dlasen bild, quod is advocat, se clihnend-ye proscher id kier, skwit attentive-ye. En ids mathmoun: "Dr. Jekyll porct namos ei Maw pharmacia. Is ei sigwrt id senst proba hant dughen bei est impur ed mutlak neneudet pro eys present wan. Unte wetos 18—, Dr J. kieup un wassime wakel bei Maw pharmacia. Is prehct hoyd kem id Maw pharmacia paurska diligentst-ye, ed sei ei etileikwt lyt ios sam qualitat, kem id yeisa fauran ei. Id cost ne importet. Tod product

est pro Dr. J. uns kheptenn exceptional ahammiyat." Tetro hieb id brev liten destull tawrlien, bet her samt un stayg spieuter ios penn, id emotion ios autor se hieb muct. Is hieb nascriben: "Bihakkillah, trehfte ghi sem tos prever product!"

"Tod est un stragno note," iey Ustad Utterson; ed tun skarp-ye, "Kam tar habte yu gwohmen do lises to?"

"Is pharmacia employeit tem grasbaniesc de id, Ustad, quem is xubh id tsay kye me kamsei to esiet es' mergis!" jawieb Poole.

"To est indubitable-ye id khat ios doctor, ne?" nabahsit is advocat.

"Lika mohn ioswo," iey is khadim destull skeud-ye; ed tun, med alto ton, "Bet id khat ne importet, chunke ho vis iom!"

"Yu vis iom?" repetihsit Ustad Utterson. "Ed tun?"

"Aurte ghi!" iey Poole. "Io hieb entret fujatan id amphitheatre, ex id bustan. Is hieb sollt snehge extro po id product, we po alyogvonc; idghi dwer ios practis eet ghyanen, ed is eet ye alter bors ios kielken, obsokend bayna ia schischees. Kun io gwohm, is spohc ub, emiss un genis schaki crie, ed mwaungsousit unte id drab do id practis. Ho vis iom unte tik oin minute, bet mien kays ghohrs ub. Saycte mi, Ustad, sei is esiet mien mayster, ma eys enokw eet masct? Sei is esiet mien mayster, ma hat is emitten tod ratcrie, ed ma hat is mwaungsoun kun is vis me? Ho serven destull diutos, ed…" Ed is wir tieyc ed kohl sien lige apter sien hand.

"Ta quant sont meg stragna circumstances," iey Ustad Utterson, "bet mehno bighabo. Vies mayster, Poole, est alnos lambhen ab oin tom siugen qua bo torture ed dusforme el victim; tois, tant quem gnohm, id alteration os

eys voc; tois, id mask kay vergihes sien nityens; tois eys las kay trehve tod pharmac, quosmed so orm atmen gweupt sem speh os ultim ganeisen—Div kwehrtu mae is biht decept! En mien explication; est kafi trauric, Poole, yaghi, ed gargic dyeitu; lakin est alnos natural, suahanct com, ed leudhert nos ex quant exorbitant alarmes."

"Ustad," iey is majordomo, pelupoikascend do pallor, tel ject ne eet mien mayster ed to est id druve. Mien mayster —tun ambhglaz is ed bikwohster—est buland, pletwost, menxu so eet quasi un dwergh." Utterson tentit proteste. "O Ustad," cricit Poole, "mehnte yu io ne gnohm mien mayster pos dwogim yars? Mehnte yu ne recogneihiem eys cap in id practis, quer ho viden iom cada aghyern miens gwit? No, Ustad, tel ject apter id mask naiwo buit Dr. Jekyll—Div woid quo eet, bet buit naiwo Dr. Jekyll; ed mien kerd beidt me od un maurdh buit commiss."

"Poole," jawieb is advocat, "sei yu saycte to, tun mien dohlg est swekwehre de. Hois meg eiskwo gahabe ia khisses vosters mayster, ciois meg stauno de tod note quod kwehct pruves is dar gwivt, io aym mien dohlg instundes tod dwer."

"Ah, Ustad Utterson, tod est un gohd decision!" cricit is majordomo.

"Ed nun gwehm' dwoter question," nabahsit Utterson. "Quoter vaht kwehre to?"

"Ma? Yu ed ego, Ustad," buit id aunpaur jawab.

"Meg suasayct," respons is advocat; "ed quodkwe siet gwehme tetos, siem pliehge mae sessiet vies fault."

"Est un pelk in id amphitheatre," etimlu Poole; "ed yu maghte ghende id cucin koistrank pro vosswo."

Is advocat ghens tod rustic yed gwaurod instrument in hand, ed subpohnd id. "Woid yu, Poole," iey is, spehcend

ub, "od yu ed ego sa-dehmos nos do un position os sem perile?"

"Kamghi yu saycte, Ustad," jawieb is majordomo.

"Tamam, smadghi ses frank," iey alter. "Wey bo mehn-mos meis quem hams saygen; maeti smad kehle ject ad mutu. Habte yu recognihn tom masken individu yu dyohrc?"

"Kay sayge ver, Ustad, to tyohc oku, ed tel creature eet tem dwibugh' quem ne kassamiem pro to. Bet sei yu maynte: kwe eet Poti Hyde?... Yaghi, credeihm eet is! Vidte yu, is hieb takriban id sam pletwos, ed hieb id sam elangver ed agil gwayt; eti quel alyis habiet ghohdt penetre unte id dwer ios laboratorium? Mae myehrste, Poti, od unte id crime, is dar hieb id cleich bi se. Bet to ne est hol. Ne woidim, Ustad Utterson, kweter yu aiwo ghiet tom Poti Hyde?"

"Sighi," jawieb is advocat. "Ho balbelt oins con iom."

"Tun yu sollte tem suawoide quem weysmee od eet semjec' skeir de tom gentleman—semjec' quod supih vos—Ne sagvo druve-ye explie als quem katha: ant iom anghen khiss kam kenos ed srigos in sien mozg."

"Admitto ho khissen kam yu descripte," iey Ustad Utterson.

"Yaghi, Ustad," jawiebit Poole. "Tun, quando so genis masc' kiep gwohl ex bayna ia chemicals ed se precipitit do id practis, to hat glohdjen mien spina. Gnohmghi to est neid pruv, Ustad Utterson; som kafi alim pro woide to; bet mensci hant irschi khisses, ed kassamiem ep id Bible eet Poti Hyde!"

"Tamam," iey is advocat. "Mien baysas me incline kyid sam point. Baym est ghi khitert in tod re. Druve-ye vos credeihm; credeihm so orm Harry buit nicen; ed credeihm

eys maurdher (po quod tik Div woid) dar lant in id kamer siens victim. Smadghi kwines! Kalte Bradshaw."

Is kyust ambikwol gwohm, meg pall ed nerveus.

"Meudhte ub, Bradshaw," iey is advocat. "Tod suspense, woidim, est muschkil quantims; lakin smos gwaukan de finihes id. Poole ed ego, weysmee vahms enbrehge do id practis. Sei in druve neid hat lit skeir, som kafi sudehn pro behre ids hol massoulia. Yed, ib est hakan sem khitert, we ibo sem yakonien tentet skape aptos, geirte pri id kantun con iom cucinpwarn, ieter wagherghesor, ed stahsiete wakht ant id dwer ios laboratorium. Vos dahms dec minutes, kay joine vies walsa."

Kun Bradshaw likwit, is advocat spohc sien saat. "Ed nun, Poole, smad joine nosters," iey is; ed ghendus id koistrank sub sien brakh, is proghieng do id aula. Ia nebhs hieb kowpen ant id meun, itak ye tod saat hieb hol nohkwn. Id wind, quod niek tod trebenschakhto tik samt intermittent kaugs, krampihsit id flicker ios kier; yed bad ies endergwohm do id amphitheatre, quer ies sess kay intizare silent. Londons grand rumor ambilud; bet prokwer eet id silence tik rupt ab un gigwahndo stieupblosk ep id pelp ios practis.

"It ghanct is unte id hol dien, Ustad," susurit Poole; "ya ed hatta unte id miers' part ios noct. Es' lyt mukhlat tik qua is dact un nov proba ex id pharmacia. Is tehrpt ses druve-ye dusmenos kay ses un solg peind os rahat! O Ustad, quel woid an stieupt in cruor? Bet kleute iter, lyt proscher— dehte vies kerd do vies aurs, Ustad Utterson, ed saycte mi, kwe est id gwayt ios doctor?"

Ia stieups cliengheer ninelangver, ed quasi-dansanta nespekent ir lentor: ia se enderkwit alnos ud Henry Jekylls

gwaurod ed swehner ghang. Utterson kwohster ed sprohg: "Biht aiw alyoject aurt?"

Poole nuk, ed antwohrd: "Si, tik oins. Oins ho io aurt iom plange."

"Plange? Quod maynte yu?" nasprohg is advocat, fauran lahn ab un horrorkreus.

"Plange kam un gwen au un lusen atmen," iey is major-domo. "Mien kerd hat tem aghnuet quem ioschi proe-plangiem."

Taiper hieb ia dec minutes zadohnen. Poole exdohlv id pelk ex ender un kowp os packkalm; id kier buit posen ep id prokwsto table kay beluces iens unte id attaque; ed, enderwaurgend ir annem, bo stohmb prosch id loco quer tod stieup eegigwaht aunmalal unte id sakwnia tos noct.

"Jekyll," Utterson kiel jahar, "io demande vide vos." Is pausit unte uno moment, yed ei gwohmit neid jawab. "Vos mauno prabh-ye, noster suspecens sont sbuden, tehrbo vide vos ed siem vide vos: sei ne per beiden, to sessiet als… Sei ne khalal tun med gvalt."

"Utterson," cricit id voc, "bihakkillah, rahimatte!"

"To ne est Jekylls voc… sontern os Hyde!" scricit Utterson. "Vrehnte id dwer, Poole!"

Ed Poole swohng id pelk uper sien oms; id cuttum udcliengh unte id hol treb, ed id rudhserge dwer se protiestus ei sclud ed ibs mifussals. Ex id practis gwohl un gjianheul, uns alnos animal garg. Id pelk buit swohngyet, ed iter ia panells crieck ed id futra sprud. Quars buit tus, bet id dreu eet kaurd ed id stolarwehrg solid. Bad ye id penkto cutt buit id demoliht sclud rohven ed fiell id dwerdebris entro ep id kelim.

Ies belaghrers, intimidet ab ir wi thambra ed id sehkwnd silence, lyt kung ed spohc do id practis quod se anac irims

97

okwims sub id enpace luce ios lampe. Un sell ogwn pricklit in id vatra, id chaykattil sohngv sieno merig melodia, oin au dwo liachics eent ghyanen, papiers suardehn ep id scribtable, ed prokwer id ogwn, id chaybestehg: ploisko ia chemicals apter schibs, hol tengicit id communsto sakwn kyal os London honoct.

Medsu terkye lyohg un peigher-ye vreinkus ed dar srehtend wirnayv. Stohmbeer proscher ep pedak, volvihr id ep ids regv ed dyir id lige os Edward Hyde. Is vohs vesters meg pior plaut pro iom, vesters ios mege ios doctor; ia traits os eys face dar tickeer samt gwit, bet uns quasi-linkwus gwit; ed ob id craspen phial in eys hand ed id akster odor om bitter mendels quod swohbh in id air, Utterson wois od is eet spehcend id nayv os uno swoneicer.

"Hams gwohmen pior sert," iey is skeud-ye, "kweter pro salve we punihes. Hyde se hat perikwiht; ed nos etileikwt tik trehve id nayv os vies mayster."

Id for mierer portion ios treb eet occupet ab id amphi-theatre, quod plehsit quasi id hol grundetage ed eet belucen ubtos, ed ab id practis, quod skip un uber etage ye uter end ed uperspohc id aula. Un corridor yug id amphi-theatre ei dwer kyid niebstrad; eti, id practis eet gwahim seni pon tod unte dwoter drab. Eent plurschi deuska schranks ed un vast kellar. Vasya buir tun rlienxien-ye prichohxt. Ielg men schranko nieudh tik ein glanez, ar quanta eent tuich ed, yeji id duil quod nifiell kata ir dwers, neid ex ia hieb esen ghyanen diutos. Id de kellar eet empediset ab un kowp raymen items, pleisten tarikhend ex id zaman ios chirurgios pre Jekyll; bet just ghyanus id dwer bihr ies warnti de mae wane etichehxtum, dank id fall uns compactios gawohbhos arankyen, qua hieb wetsois inter-

dehn gwahe in. Neidloc buit vis trace os Henry Jekyll, kweter mortu au gwiv.

Poole stiemp ep ia flises ios corridor. "Is sollt ses begrabht ter," iey is akowsiend-ye id clangh.

"Autah is hat mwaungsoun," iey Utterson. "Ed is abgwahsit chehxtum id dwer kyid niebstrad. Id eet andamt; ed meg prokwem, wohs un rustpoiko cleicho lyehgend ep ia flises.

"Id ne tengiet meg daughe," kieusit is advocat.

"Daughe?" repetih Poole. "Ne vidte yu, Ustad, od id es' vrohnc' kamsei anghen habiet valct id med sien takoun?"

"Yaghi," bahsit Utterson, "ed hatta ia brehgpoints sont berust." Bo wirs oispohc mutu, hayran. "To udghap' me, Poole," iey is advocat. "Smad rikes id practis."

Stigheer silent ubdrabs, ed dar samt waurmen-ye yazgost glanez kyid nayv, tyic un rlienxiener perichehxen ios mathmoun ios practis. Ep oin table eent traces os chemic wehrg, variat miden kowps os sem albh saldo lyict ep glasdiejis, kamsei is biedan wir habiet esen interrupen unte un experiment.

"Tod est id sam drogh quem quo io semper eebringho ei," iey Poole, ed sammel kun is bahsit, id chaykattil spreudih iens yehsstridend-ye.

To volgih iens kyid vatra, prosch quos wierme id foteuylo hieb esto tract, samt id chaybestehg ye prayghest, con hatta suker in id tasse. Un gjia tohl oik jasamats; oin ex ia lyohgit ghyanto nieb id chaytepji, ed Utterson recognih ter hayran sem exemplar unios maarifkitab, de quod Jekyll hiebit pelus wohkwn samt kehnsen, ed taiper annoten, wihandic-ye, samt pamrlaneihnd blasphemies.

Poskwo in id druna irios revue tos kyal, ies sokars gwohm ant id enebspecule, do quos dubes ies oispohc samt

involuntar horror. Bet id eet wohrt yoitkwe id ibs dik neid ploisko id subpemb diutis leikend subter id tavan, id ogwn tweisend do centen repetitionen engwn ia schibs iom glasalmarn, ed ir wi pall ed bayasen firasats clihn kyira reflects.

"Tod specule hat vis stragna jects, Ustad," susurit Poole.

"Bet id hat vis neid stragner quem sien wi presence her," jawieb is advocat samt id sam ton. "Quodghi Jekyll kwohr—" Is interrup samt un spreud, dind kardehvso sien sliebe: "Kaytar Jekyll tohrb un enebspecule?"

"Yu daumte prabh!" iey Poole.

Poskwo ies vols kyid orbatstable. Ep id, bayna suardeht schids, uperlyohg un plaut vulbh quod bohr, in id khat ios doctor, id nam os Ustad Utterson. Is advocat dissgillit id, ed plur inner vulbhs fiell ep id podloga. Id prest eet un volscriben, redact med ia sam excentric lexis quem tod is hieb dahn tsay six munts prever, ed dehlgend daughe ka testament in fall os mohrt, ed os act os donation in fall os disparition, yed tayus id nam Hyde; is advocat lis ter, samt indescriptible staunos, sien nam Gabriel John Utterson. Spohcit preter Poole, dind iter id papier, ed bad iom defuncto criminalo lyehgend ep id pelppodloga.

"Dusasco," iey is. "Is behans to hol unte ta quant akhir diens. Is hieb neid raison os liubhes me, is sollit irasce ob se vide evict, lakin is ne hat destrugen tod document."

Is ghens id senst papier: eet un cort bild handscript ab iom doctor, samt un tarikhe heruper. "Oh, Poole," scricit is advocat, "is eet her, ed gwiv, hoydkye. Is khac' dis-pareihvs unte tem pau: is soll' dar gwive, is soll' mwaung-soue?... Yed ma fuges? Ed quosmed? In tod fall maghmos wey venture ad kale to un suicide? Oh, tehrbmos kaure.

103

Prekheisso maghiemos yed involve vies mayster do sem jalnic catastrophe."

"Ma yu ne leiste, Ustad?" sprohg Poole.

"Ob baym," jawieb is advocat solenn-ye. "Div comprehendtu baym aun cause!" Ed poskwo is brigh id papier kye sien okwi ed lis quo sehkwt:

> "Mien kyar Utterson,—Quando to pehdsiet inter vies ghesors, habsiem disparihn, unte qua circumstances ne ho tjwowschi kay gvaedde, bet mien instinct ed vasya circumstances miens aunnam situationios mi sayge id fin est sure ed od niet kunges. Adieu ad vos, ed plais preter leiste id narn de quod Lanyon mi hat warnt ei eet zaruri uperdahe ad vos; ed sei yu kaurte de etiwoide, anagnohte ghi id confession os
>> "Vies newirtic ed biedan prient,
>>> "HENRY JEKYLL."

"Kwe eet un trit vulbh?" sprohg Utterson.

"Her, Ustad," iey Poole, ed ei uperdehsit un taungh sgillmoinihn document.

Is advocat snig id do sien gep. "Niem sayge jec' dayir tod papier. Sei vies mayster hat fugen we mohrn, maghmos bariem salve eys kleumen. Est nun dec saat: vahm gwirlaye ed lises in pace ta documents; yed gwehmsiem tsay pre midnoct, ed tun vansiemos id police."

Sielgeer, andamus pos se id dwer ios amphitheatre; ed Utterson, linkwnd iter slougs samghat ambh id ogwn in id vestibule, gwahsit sien bureau kay lises ia dwo narns quer is sollit bad vrehe id explication ios mysteir.

CAPITEL IX

ID NARN AB DOCTOR LANYON

Dieno 9 Januar, yani quar diens prever, io diek per id vespernehmen un recommanden post, handscript ab mien collegh ed prever scoldust Henry Jekyll. Io meg stieun de, ar wey nel-ye swohd nos yises brevs; io hieb viden iom, hieb hatta dinnern con iom ye id prever vesper; ed concepim in nies relations neid quod miegh justifie id formalitat uns talg maktub. Id mathmoun tos brev ieug mien surprise; idghi arohg tod werden:

"Dien 10 Januar 18—
"Mien kyar Lanyon,—Ste oino mienen veutst prients; ed quayque hams yando differto de scientific questions, iosmee khako mehme sem brehg in nies winmenos.Naiwo buit un dien quando, sei yu mi habiete sayct: 'Jekyll, mien gwit, mien honor, mien aum, depende vos,' ne habiem maulen mien bayga au mien levter hand kay hehlpe vos. Ar Lanyon, honoct, mien gwit, mien honor, mien aum sont quanta ye vies mercie; sei yu vos forprehpte ud me, som lust. Yu ghehdiete suppones, pos tod preface, od vahm budes vos ad semject deshonoranto mehghtu. Kehnste ab vosswo.

"Wehlo vos hoane voster ceter homologhias pro honoct—esdi yu esiete kyuken ei trem os un cesar; emte un fiaker, nibo vies wi wogh est fauran behandet; ed samt tod brev in hand ka reference, gwahte seid-ye do mien dom. Poole, mieno majordomo, hat sien wehlens; yu trehfsiete iom skehptend vies arriven con un schlesser. Sessiet tun zaruri vrehnge id dwer miens practis; ed yu mon siete entre, ghyane id glasalmar (buksteiv E) levi, hatta dwinghend-ye id sclud sei est andamt; ed extrage, *samt ids hol mathmoun kam yu vrehsiete id*, id quart liachic topptos wa trit budtos. In id extreme gjian quer wehsmi, morbid-ye baym an vahm dusnihes vos; bet esdi rhalto, yu recogneihsiete tod liachic dank ids mathmoun: oik pulvers, un phial ed un papier cadern. Tod liachic io iltije ke yu behrte tsay con vos do Cavendish Square exact-ye kam yu habsiete vrehn id.

"Tod est preter part ios service: en dwoter. Yu solliete gwirlayus, sei yu abgwahte yant yu habte daken tod brev, diu pre midnoct; bet prefero vos linkwes tod prist, ne tik ibo tyehca semo nestambhim ni imprevisible obstacle, sontern ob est tohrben un saat kun vies khadims sessient in lict pro quo vos etileikwsiet kwehrtu. Tun ye midnoct, beudo ke yu sessiete mon in vies practis, ed ke yuswo sinsiete entre un wir qui se presentesiet in mieno nam, ed kem ei uperdehsiete id liachic yu habsiete brighto tsay ex mien wi practis. Tun yu habsiete act vies rol ed algvt mien complete gratitude. Ego saygo od pos penkwe minutes, sei yu druve-ye gnohskwte, yu habsiete ghapt od ta arrangements sont os capital importance; ed sei yu aiwo neglegiete oin tom, tem fantastic quem to maght kwehke, kad yu habsiete gurawen vies menos med mieno nehc au bariem aumgvon.

"Confident kam esmi yu mae beleicsiete mieno maidehsa, mien kerd aghnuet ed mien hando tremblet just quando mehno de. Fikerte ghi od som, ye tod saat, in un stragno steto, kikwehndend uno naudhkyehros quod neid fantasia ghehdiet ultra-imagine, ed hassa alnos consciem od, sei yu me servicet barwakt, mien troubles forswehndsient kamsei habient esen tik un fiction. Servicet me plais, mien kyar Lanyon, ed yu salvsiete

"Vies prient,

"H. J.

"P.S.: Io hieb ja sgillen tod maktub quan un nov baysa mi enfiell. Kad id baride deuyseihsiet mien plan, edghi yu niete dake tod brev pre cras aghyern. In tod fall, mien kyar Lanyon, parkwehrte tod mission kun tod vos sessiet gadabst in id druna ios dien; ed iter oins intizarte mieno messager tiel midnoct. Kad hol sessiet ja pior sert; ed sei id nocto dehnt aun nel gwehmt, woidte od yu neti vidsiete Henry Jekyll."

Leisus tod brev, io yakiniesc od mien collegh eet foll; bet esta to buit pruven trans cada dwoi, io me khiss bohnden ab kwehre kam is nieudh. Ye minter io ghieb tod farrago, ye minter io kohns-pet ids importance; ed un ithan redagen maidehsa khiek ses arct aun gwaur massoulia. Schowi stahsim ub fauran ed io stigh do un hansom quod me wohgh seid ad Jekylls dom. Is majordomos intizier mien arriven; is hieb daken ud iom sam oulako quem ego un recommanden post mathmounend bereulens ed hieb manden strax un schlesser ed un stolar. Toy bo dabers gwohmeer menxu eems dar tolkend; ed comgwahsam id prever anatomic amphitheatre os Doctor Denman, unte biht (kam yu aundwoi ja woid) aisic-ye accedden id practis

111

os Doctor Jekyll. Idso dwer eet solid, idso sclud excellent; is stolar itirief od to ei moliciet ed od is tehrbiet sauke id, sei gvalt esiet necessar; ed is schlesser lit prosch desperation. Yed senter eet un handug type, ed pos dwo hors orbat, id dwer vighyahsit. Id glasalmar E ne eet andamen; ed extraxim id liachic, quod io parvulbh in kalmo med un charsaf, dind, con tod item rikim Cavendish Square.

Ter, io skul chehxe ids mathmoun. Ia pulvers eent destull suapackt, yed ne samt id ghab uns professional pharmaceut; yoitkwe ia hieb esen okwivid-ye comdehn ab iomswo Jekyll; ed quando io ghyien oin tom sachets, io trohv quod mi kwohk ses simple kwit cristallin sald. Id phial, quei poskwo dahsim mien attention, kwecto pwolpohld med un cruorrudh liqueur samt un hog-ye akri odor quod mi tengicit mathmoune phosphor ed sem volatil ether. De alter ingredients ho io neid dayi. Id cadern eet un trivial scolcadern ed mathmounit neid meis quem un serie tarikhen. Ta spiend uper un prist maungen yars, bet observim od neideti hieb esen niscriben pon quasi oino yar, destull abrupt-ye. Her ed ter un bragv remarke niebsohkw un tarikhe, adic-ye ne meis quem oin werd; "double" prohp maghses sixens ex un total pluren centens dienen; ed oin baygh aus in id daftar ed sohkwn ab plur alamats os taajub, "total deuysen!!!" To hol, quayque to kweh mien curiositat, me sbringhih neid definitive. Her eent un phial os sem tincture, un proba os sem sald, ed id daftar os un serie om experiments qua hieb waust (kam piora om Jekylls paurskens) in neid practic utilitat. Quosmed ghohd id presence tom items affece auter id honor, id afiya, au id gwit miens fugitive collegh? Sei eys messager ghohd gwahe oin stet, ma khiek is gwahe alyo? Ed hatta suppose sem impediment, ma eet zaruri primes tom gentleman in

113

secret? Ye meis reflexim, ye stets convicter bihsim od eem deilend con un fall os cerebral siuge; ed congeidus mien khadims pro id noct, rechargim un veut revolver sei wehsiem aiw in naudhward.

Midnoct hieb just swohnt unte hol London, kun id kschong tus id dwer stump-ye. Io gwohm ad ghyane, ed trohv un desbuland wir heudelnd protie ia pillars ios portic.

"Gwehmte yu nami Dr. Jekyll?" io sprohg.

Is mi sieygit "ya", med dwighen geste; ed kun io hieb inviten iom ad entre, is me obedih tik pos glanzus retro sokar-ye kyid temos ios place. Nedalg, un policiste ieg perodh swehngend un lanterne. Ye tod vid, mi kwohk od mien visitoro trohs ed dar meis-ye spohd.

Ta sonterkweits me ubfiell, itirafo, desamat-ye; ed menxu sohkwim iom tiel id kweitert miens practis, pristahsim nudes mien gvond. Ter io bad hieb waurmen os perivide iom. Quo eet bariem yakin, eet od io ne hieb naiwo ghaten iom prever-ye. Is eet desbuland, kam ho ja sayct; eti buim ubfallt ab id repulsive expression os eys firasat, ab id exceptional aspect is pors, unios mier muscular activitat yuct uni ne minter mier apparent sliebe os constitution, ed fin-ye, ed dar meis maghses, ab id aunsam psychologic trouble quod eyso jawar mi causit subjective-ye. Tod trouble anac sem analogia con un inkapem os ankylose, ed bihsit hamraht ab semo notable slaben os puls. Ye tod moment, id anadehsim ad sem personal ed idiosyncrasic antipathia; ed stieun mer-ye de id acuitat om idsa manifestations; bet ho haben tuntos raisons os credihes od eys origin lyohg meg deuber in mieno menscbuhsa, ed tyohc ex uno motivation nobler quem haines.

So individu (qui hieb ithan, yantkye is hieb arriven, isnahn in me un curiositat quod kweitiem gairn ka dussaun)

vohs roubes qua habient kwohrno grotesk quomgvonc ordinar anghen; eysghi povestis, quayque ex un suagust godwehb, eent aunmeid-ye pior plaut pro iom unte cada meges: eys pantalono nilik ambh eysa jambs, ed id hieb esen slahno nitos mae bihe sohlken ghomi, id taylle os eys redingote wohs ender eys hanks, ed eys colnier ghyahsit weur-ye ep eys omsa. Aunsam sayctu, tod leikarisk vesdet nel-ye me wehnih glihes. Punor, dat eet in idpet buhsa ios individu qui stahsit ant me semject abnormal ed mis-gohnt—semject seizant, surprindant ed pamrlaneihnd—tod fresch disparitat kwohkit kwohrt kay bides ed kardwne mien preter khisses; quetos mien interesse de id buhsa ed pinseing tos wir, quei se addih un curiositato de eys origin, eys gwit, eys fortune ed status in id mund.

Ta remarkes qua ho tohrpto tant antplehce ter, yed dureer in mieno ment unte oik secundes. Eti rierz in mien visitor id jar os un gvero sreht.

"Habte yu id?" scricit is. "Habte yu id?" Ed in id excess os eys impatience, is gwohm do sizes mien brakh kam kay scutte me.

Touchet ab iom io khiss in mien veines un sorte os glehdjgvol. Io repuls iom. "Vedim, Poti," ieyim ei. "Yu myehrste ne ho bad habt id plaisure os bignohe vos. Plais seddte ghom, prehgo." Ed kay ei dikes id exempel, ioswo sess ghom do mien adic foteuyl sekwent mien ordinar weidos dia un sieug, tem maung-ye quem mi eet permitten ab tod sert saat, id buhsa mienen sweurghs, ed id horror so visitor mi inspirit.

"Plais pardonte me, Doctor Lanyon," jawieb is destull polite-ye. "Yu saycte alnos prabh; ed mien impatience hat udact mien politesse. Ho gwohmen hetro buden ab vies collegh, Doctor Henry Jekyll, pro un important affaire; ed

sekwent quo ho ghapt…" is interrup, ed brigh sien hand sieni gurgule, ed io ghohd vide, speit eyso sakwn attitude, is pit enderwaurge id proschgumt unios nervencollapse— "ho ghap' leit de un liachic…"

Io rahimiet id angst os mien visitor, ne minter maghses quem mien crehscend curiositat.

"En id, Poti," antwohrd io, kyeusend-ye id liachic, lyeh-gend ep id pelppodloga apter un table ed dar covohrno med id charsaf.

Is klieup kyid object, dind hielt, ed brigh sien hand do sien kerd. Io ieur id convulsive gaknaros eysen ghyanus; ed eys lige mi kwohk tem sliep quem me alarmim de to tant pro eys gwit quem pro eys aum.

"Plais ganeiste," ieyim ei.

Is mi pors un terrifiento smeih, dind, kam moven ab desperation, rohv id charsaf. Kun is vis id mathmoun, is emiss un swehner sleuct uns tem immense rehmen quem io sess petrifiet. Ed id niebst moment, med un ja swekwohrt voc, "Habte yu un meidglas?" sprohg is.

Muschkil-ye stahsim ub ed ei dahsim quo is iskwit.

Is me dienkit med uno neukend smeih, mid oika ghutts ios rudhios tincture, ed addih tetro oino iom pulverdosen. Tod mix, subrudh in-kap, bidusk, ye meis dissolven bihr ia cristalls, samt un notable effervescence, dind gwehlih smulk steumjets. Fauran tod combination zabrohn ed quasi sammel bihsit maurpurpwr, pre wehrte do glawgv. Mien visitor, qui hieb smautern ta metamorphoses med un lasni ok, smih, pos id glas ep id table, dind volgus kye me, nispohc me kam scrutend-ye.

"Nun est zaruri," iey is, "panges quo etileikwt. Sessiete yu hakime? Klues mien mayn, mi permitte ghende tod glas con me ed salge tetos aun etimlues? Autah uperwehndt vies

excess os curiositat? Mehnte pre antwehrdte, ar acsiem sekwent vies vol. Sekwent vies vol, vos linkwsiem kam yu eete prever, neter richer, ni hakimer, nib id sense de servicevs un wir in mortal danger poitt bihe hissap' ka opnos os atmen. Seighi yu preferte mane, un nov province os gnohsa ed nov avenues kye maschouria ed magh vos ghyahsient, herkye in tod kyal in oin instant; ed vies vid sessiet blins ab un kyudos quod taraghiet Satans incredulitat."

"Poti," ieyim simulend remane coul quayque io druveye ne eem it, "yu bahte med enigmas ed kad yu niete daume an remano perplex face vos. Bet ho nun kwohrn un pior deub itner bayna inexplicable services aun pause pre vido id end!"

"Gohd ghi," jawieb mien visitor. Lanyon, mehmte vies oit: quo sehkwt est sub professional secret. Ed nun, yu qui habte esen bohnden temdiu ibs anghst ed materialst mayns, yu qui habte neget id virtut os transcendental medicin, yu qui habte nays vies superiors, dyeite!"

Is brigh id glas ad sien lipps ed pohsit unte oin schtoss. Un crie udcliengh; is kharkhier, titubit, antgrip id table, ed nastahsit, samt oistarnd sehrgstrihn okwi, kwehsend ed gheisdend; ed menxu io dyi iom, credih vide in iom un change… is mi kwohk pfwehnge… ed oino moment serter io klieup ub, slahmend-ye me protie id mur, mien brakh lift kay alege ud tod kyudos, mieno ment lahn ab terror.

"Yallah!" scricim, ed "O Yallah!" Semper iter; terghi ant mien okwi—pall ed scutten ed pwolbayaldissen, ed ambhtastend ant se med sien hands, kam un scrisct mensc—ter stahsit Henry Jekyll!

Quo is mi sieyg unte id niebst hor, khako niscribe id. Ho viden quo ho viden, ho aurn quo ho aurn, ed mien atmen

est sieug ob to; ed hatta nun kun tod vid hat swohnden ex mien okwi, daumo kwe credeihm id, ed khako antwehrde. Mien gwit est alnos taraghen; swehpen me hat likwt; yawm-ye me hantet un katelst terror; kheisso mien ajal sagwehmt ed od mehrsiem; yed mehrsiem incredule. Dayir id moral turpitude so wir mi hat auncovohrn, hatta pos kionkudakrus, khako, hatta in memoria, gwive con id aun un horrortrehs. Saycsiem tik oin, Utterson, ed to (sei yu aiwo maghiete credihes id) sessiet meis quem kafi. So gohnos qui rep do mien dom ye tod noct eet, sekwent Jekylls wi confession, gnoht sub id nam Hyde ed aptersoct unte id holo land ka maurdher os Carew.

HASTIE LANYON

Capitel X

Henry Jekylls Hol Bayan ios Re

Gnahsim anno 18—, samt un large fortune ed excellent ghabs, uns industrieus buhsa, muadeb dia hakimes ed sell bayna mien sokwis, ed it, kam miegh ses supposen, samt quant garantie uns honorable ed mumtase gwit. Yed mien khiterst fault buit un certain impatient suamenos, quodghi hat noroctiht maungs, bet kam talg ho pohndt kaurd ad reconcilye con mien dasturic desire os tines mien cap hog, ed os endue in public un graver wajkho quem quiskwe. Tetos resultit od me levrim ad plaisure tik in secret, ed od kun io niek id oumer os aumia, ed inkiep ambhspehce ed vighabe mien progressa ed mien situation in societat, mi eet ja dwight un profundo duplicitat os existence. Meis quem oinis habiet glihto de ia ambi-gheumens quommed io vinovatiesc; men kata ia ideal hoges qua io mi hieb pact, dyisim ed kohl ia samt un quasi maraz schamkhisses. Idghi tyrannic kweitu mienen aspirations, meg petis quem besonters depravet eakias, me buwit quo som ed, med un deuber tomos quem bi pleist menscens, separit in me ta xeimens om sellt ed khitert quer se nehmt ed quommed wardht id double buhsa im adams.

In mien particular fall, buim brighen ad mimehne intense-
ye de tod kaurd loy os existence quod enderkeiht religion
ed quod skeipt oino iom abundantst aziyatsurcen. Nespekent mien hol duplicitat, io dohbh nel-ye bihe namen
un hypocrite: mien bo gons eent kathalika uns perfect
sinceritat; eem ne meis ioswo quando rejexim dwinegh ed
mers do eakia, quem quando io mi udorbiet, uperdien, id
weida quod rehmt peins ed gvols. Ed wakyet od id sehkw
om mien scientific studyes, alnos orientet kyuno mystic ed
transcendanto genos, reieg ed projexit un akster luce ep id
dayi io hieb de tod aiwic weir inter mien constitutive
elements. Ex dien do dien, ed ex bo gons os mien intelligence, id moral ed id intellectual, io katha lit proscher tod
druve, quos partial aunstehgen me hat dribhen do un tem
dekhschatic naufrage: odnu mensc ne est druve-ye oin,
sontern druve-ye dwo. Saygo dwo, ob id stand om mien wi
gnohsas ne strehct trans. Alyi men sehkwsient, alyi me
udwoidsient, ed deurso tarke od mensc sessiet gnohn ab un
pohltos em multiforme, heterogene ed independent peri-
kwehlers. Ego de, ob id buhsa mien gwit, lit perodh
infallible-ye in oin direction ed tik in oin direction. Ye id
moral gon, ed in mien wi person, od io uc recognihes id
complete ed primitive buhsa'l mensc; io vis od, ex ia dwo
personalitats qua chid po id camp os mien conscience, sei
io ghohd prabh-ye bihe ayt ka uter au alter, to gwohm ex
od eem bund-ye bo; ed ab un apank tarikhe, baygh pre id
sehkw om mien scientific soks mi hieb hatta enderskaut id
piernst possibilitat uns talg miracle, io hieb ucen pinwes
majnoun-ye, kam un bell sogn, id project os separe ta
constitutive elements. Sei ieter, io mi sieyg, ghehdiet tik
bihe bewict in separen identitats, gwit bihiet rohmen ex
quantum eet dusbohr; el neprabh kwehriet sien itner,

ludhert ex ia aspirations ed mentangst es sien meis adil yem; ed el prabh ghehdiet bad progredde darm-ye ed gwaukan-ye unte sien ieun, kwehrnd ia ikhsans in qua el vrehsit sien plaisure, ed neti exposen ibs disgrace ed kionku causen ab tod rhayir khitert. Pro id kyasen os menscgenos buit tod incoherent fasco samghaten yoitkwe eni un dohrn conscience ti witer yems ithan dayim jidale protie mutu. Kwe ne ghohd i bihe dissocyen?

Io hieb ithan duben do mien reflexions quando, kam ho sayct, un gonluce inkiep illumine tod subject pon id laboratorium table. Bikwahsim dar profunder quem buit aiwo bayanen id tremblant immaterialitat, id mighel-lik transience tos kwecto tem solid corpos quod dums. Io aunstohg od sem agents ghehde attaque tod krewosvulbh ed rehve id kam wind ayrt ia pans uns delt. Yed niem lites dalger do tod scientific part miens confession, bi dwo dohbra sababs. Preter, ob ho matht ye mien expense od id calamiteus behrmen nosters gwit est bohndt proaiw ibs omsims al mensc, ed sei biht piten rejece id, id reict samt infamiliarer ed horribler pressem. Dwoter, ob kam mien bayan way expliesiet pior aweis, mien aunstehgens eent incomplete. Kafi, tun, kay io ne tik recognih in mieno natural corpos id mer aura ed semject samlik ei emanation iom forcen qua skeipe mieno ment, somdehsim un producto dank quod ta forces ghohd beghsasce ir suprematia, ed bihe tayt ab un dwoter apparent forme, ne minter representative miens ego, chunke id eet id expression ed bohr id gnohmen om niter elements os mien atmen.

Io kung diu pre empraxise tod theoria. Io pior wois od riskim nehc; unghi solg drogho quod tem staur-ye controlit ed tariegh idpet poli os identitat, ghohd unte id lytst kaghlit uns overdose au ob id lytsto duswaurmen in sien applica-

tion abolihes alnos tod immaterial badan quod id changihskwim. Bet id tentation uns tem aunsam ed profund aunstehgen fin-ye upertreh ia alarme znaycs. Io hieb diutos preparet mien tincture; io pakyiev unte oins, ex un pharmaceutic firma, un large quantitat uns particular sald quod gnohsim, ex mien experiments, ka id sensto naudht ingredient; ed sert unte un balstohmen noct, comdehsim ia elements, smieuter ia yehse ed comdumes in id glas, ed quando ia hieb zabrohnt, samt uno nert gwehl os courage, expohsim id potion.

Io spruv ia keapayst aziyats: un grehnden om mien osta, uno mortal nausea, ed un agonia os atmen quod neter gnahsa ni mohrt ghehdt periese. Dind, jaldi, ta tortures oiswohnd, ed io ganis kam ex un grave siuge. Eet semjecto stragn in mien sensations, semject indescriptible-ye nov, ed ex todpet jadidia, incredible-ye swadh. Io khiss yuner, legver, norocter in mien corpos; eet in me un capic effrenation, un aunaurdhen flutt sensualen kwitern per mien imagination kam un assania druna, un dissolution iom diemens os obligation, uno negnoht yed ne innocent lure ios atmen. Io khiss, yant id prest annem mienios novios gwit, meis peigher, decs meis peigher, persclawt ab mien khiter orinstincts; ed tod bren tunkye medv ed delectit me kam vin. Io strohc mien brakhs, charmt ab id freschia tom sensations; ed iosmed fauran insiefim od mien stature hieb schrohnken.

Eet neid specule, ye tod tarikhe, in mien kyal; quod oistaht nieb me menxu scribo buit brighto tetro serter ed pro tapet transformations. Noct, lakin, eet ja maurg… ed tod maurg, speit sien temos, vahsit moxu gehne dien… i weikers miens baytel eent deubst-ye swehpend, ed io karrier, hol gururic kam io eem med speh ed triumph,

venture in mien nov skeip tem dalgtro quem do mien kamer. Io tohr id aula, quer warwntos ia constellations me nispohc staunos-ye, me iom prest creature tos genos quod ir aunswehpen wakht ibs viskieu; io snohg unte ia corridors, tarnien in mien wi hem; ed, ghehdus do mien kamer, io vis ye id prest ker id kwehkia os Edward Hyde.

Dehlgo bahe her tik per theoria, saygend ne quo io woid, sontern quo suppono ses probablest. Id khiter gon miens buhsa, quei io hieb transfern id efficient pinseing, eet minter robust ed minter antplohcto quem id sellst io hieb just rejecen. Eti, in id druna miens gwit, quod hieb esen, pos hol, nev decdels uns gwit om effort, virtut ed control, id hieb esen pelu mins kmehn. Ed hois io vighieb od Edward Hyde eet tem meg desbulander, slancer ed yuner quem Henry Jekyll. Kam sellt se inikies ep uters firasat, khitert alnos wierdh ep alters traits. Khitert, eti, (quer persisto vide id merti gon al mensc), hiebit prect tod corpos med dusformitat ed decheance. Yed, kun tod biaur effigie mi prohp in id specule, io spruv ne repulsion, sontern meg petis un sympathia elan. Soschi eet ego. Is mi kwohk natural ed mensc. Mienims okwims pors is un intenser incarnation os spirit, is bevis integraler ed oiner quem id imperfect ed composite apparence quod io hieb tuntro kwit mieno. Ed in to, io indubitable-ye mohn prabh. Ho observen od, kun enduim id enokw os Hyde, nimen ghohd gwehme prosch me aun visible prekhisses in sien krewos. To, kam id kwahm, eet ob vasyi ensans, kam i ghatmos, sont comdeht ex sellt ed khitert: ed Edward Hyde, mon in ia rangs os menscgenos, eet pur khitert.

Io kung unte tik oino minute ant id specule: mi eet dar zaruri tente dwoter conclusive experiment; etilikwit vide an io hieb lust mien identitat trans redemption ed dohlg

fuges pre fajer ex un dom quod neti esiet mieno; ed spehdus do mien practis, iter oins preparim ed expohsim un glas, io iter oins payss ia aziyats os dissolution, ed iter oins ganisim samt id pinseing, id stature ed id lige os Henry Jekyll.

Ye tod noct hieb io nact id fatal crucen. Habiem io hassilet mien aunstehgen samt un nobler spirit, habiem io risken id experiment sub id waldh om genereus au zakir aspirations, hol habiet esen als, ed per ta agonias om mohrt ed gnahsa, me habiem buwen un angel instet un demon. Id drogh hieb neid selective action; eet neter diabolic ni divin; id tik dwigh ia dwers ios karcer skipt ab mieno menos, ed, instar iens captives os Philippi, quoy eent eni antsals. Ye tod zaman, mien virtut rafliet; mien eakia, budt ab ambition, buit alertet ed prompt ad brunges id waurmen; ed quo buit gwehliht buit Edward Hyde. Hois, quayque ho habto dwo pinseings tem quem dwo kwehkias, uter eet alnos khiter, ed alter eet dar is veut Henry Jekyll, so heterogene composit quom desperim diutos de reforme au kayjine. Id movment eet schowi alnos kye meis khiter.

Hatta ye tod tid hieb io ne bad hassilet mien aversion kye teursia uns gwit os studye. Eem dar yando suamenos dia glewos; ed dat mien plaisures eent (kay sayge id lytst) pau alt, ed dat, ne tik eem suagnoht ed suadyit, sontern io atiesc, tod incoherence miens gwit bihsit cadadien meis dusgwohmen. Ep cid gon tentit me mien nov magh hina bihsim persclawt. Io tohrb tik pohe id scharab, kay spolye fauran id corpos ios maschourios professor, ed kay endue, kam un teug mantel, tod os Edward Hyde. Smihsim ant tod dayi, pohndim id tun glewost; ed io pliohg samt meticuleusst kaur. Io stiejer ed meublim tod Soho dom, quetro Hyde buit ighnuet ab id police, ed engagim ka

135

gouvernante un creature quam suawoisim ses silent ed inscrupuleus. Eti, io mohld mienims khadims od fulan Poti Hyde (quom im descripsim) habiet plen lure ed magh in mien dom ana id place; ed kay im familiarihes tom person, kay vergihes hadthas, miswo kyukim hem mien dwoter person. Poskwo io redieg tod testament quod vos tem pelu scandalisit; yoitkwe sei aiwo semject ghyalir mi wakyiet ka Doctor Jekyll, ghehdiem nagwive ka Edward Hyde aun financialo leus. It ubbohrgen, kam io suppos, bachimien, io bibrug ia stragn immunitats miens position.

Xiawngja leuds eehoyernt centengs kay dostringes ira crimes, menxu ir wi person ed kleumen remien schala-schen. Buim quantenprest qui ieg it pro sien plaisures. Buim is prest qui ghohd it prehpe in umum samt nerencausable respectabilitat, ed qui pos uno moment, kam un scolpwarn, ghohd oisdue ta launvesters ed merge capo perodh do id mar os lure. Bet pro me, in mien impenetrable mantel, mien salvtat eet complete. Mehnte de—ne hatta existim! Io tohrb tik entre mien laboratorium, oik secundes kay prepare ed sorbe id scharab quod io mi semper behandih; ed quodkwe is forfiec, Edward Hyde swohnd kam solukbuhar ep un specule; ed ter vice iom, sakwn-ye hemi, studyend sub id midnoct lampe, un wir quom suspecens ne miegh strifes, eet vrehno nimen meis quem Henry Jekyll.

Ia plaisures qua io spohd ad paurske in mien desguise eent, kam ho sayct, pau alt, mae use un strehnger lexis. Bet in ia ghesors os Edward Hyde, mox biwohrteer do monstrueus. Quan eereiko ex ta excursions, eem ops mers in un genos os daumos dia mien wekalatsdepravitat. So familiar demon quom io kyuk ex mien wi atmen ed quom io yis mon kay is kwohr ad sien libitum, eet un inherent-ye

137

khiter ed vilain ses; quantum is ieg ed mohn eet centren ep iomswo; is kwecto drohnk plaisure samt gverlas cada degree os torture protiev alyem, zalim ed petrakerd. Henry Jekyll yando ghisd ant ia agsa ab Edward Hyde; bet tod situation, skapend ordinar loys, ed insidieus-ye slimber eys conscience. Eet Hyde, pos hol, ed Hyde mon, qui eet vinovat. Jekyll ne khiteriesc ob to; kun eegehrt, so eevreht sien sell quantitats okwivid-ye intact; is hatta eespehdt, bilkull, ad diskwehre id khitert Hyde hieb kwohrt. Ed it nierc eys conscience.

Ne gjuchienskwo ia agsa quom complice bihsim (ar hatta nunkye pau kwahm committus ia). Tik deicskwo her ia warnens ed successive etapes qua mierk id proschgumt miens kyasen. Buit preter un lytil aventure quod dribh neid consequence ed quod siem grance me ad udwekwne. Un crueltatagos protiev un bent attraxit kye me id grasban uns passant, quom io recognih serter ses vies cousin; is liek ed i parents ias magv joineer iom; buir minutes kun io biey de mien gwit; ed fin-ye, kay sutes iro prabhst ressentiment, ad Edward Hyde buit dwighto duce iens tiel Henry Jekylls dwer ed ibs uperdahe ka payghen un cheque tragen in id nam os Henry Jekyll. Yed tod danger buit facil-ye eliminen pro id future, ghyanend-ye un conto in alyo bank in id nam iosswo Edward Hyde; ed kun, rogyend-ye mien wi khat, io hieb dadwt un signature mieni double, io mohn io wohs exter id schaecheing os fat.

Takriban dwo munts pre id maurdh os Sir Danvers, io hieb salgen pro oino mienen aventures, hieb gwirlayto ye un sert saat, ed gohr ye id niebsto dien in crovat samt semkam rhayr-adic sensations. In vain io ambispohc; in vain io vis id sober meublar, ed ia vast proportions miens appartment ios place; in vain io recognih tant id wardh ios

mahogany miens crovat quem id ambhriss iom cortins; semject mi ee-sisigwrit ne eem quer io credih ses, sontern inkye id smulk Soho kamer quer eeswehpo in Edward Hydes cuit. Io nays meswo, ed ka gohd psycholog, bipieursk indolent-ye ia causes tos illusion, ed sammel prist-ye me likw ei amat aghyernraflat. Eem it besic, quan, unte oino mienen meis oisbuden moments, mien ok viglaz mien hand. Taiper id hand os Henry Jekyll (kam yu habte ops kaut) eet professional in skeip ed mege: eet plaut, darm, albh ed khauris. Bet id hand io tun vis, kafi clar-ye, in id gehlbo luce uns aghyern ios medyios os London, tod hand pwolcraspend id charsaf eet punor maigher, gneubhic, samt vidil veines, uns ghomlik pallor ed dens-ye weulost. Eet Edward Hydes hand.

Abstauniht, sturdiht, dyisim id unte un wassime pwol-minute, pre terror sbud eni me, tem brusk ed spreudeihnd quem un crasch om cymbals; ed klaupend ex mien crovat, io rusch kyid specule. Ant id vid quod mien okwi dahr, mien sehrg buit changen do semject aunfin-ye teun ed glehdjic. Yaghi, io hieb lyohcto ghom ka Henry Jekyll, ed staht ub ka Edward Hyde. Quosmed ghohd to bihe expliet? Io dieum; ed tun, samt alyo terrorskac—quosmed ghohd to bihe remiden? Id aghyern eet ja sert, i khadims ambikwohl; mien quanta droghs lyohg in id practis, ed kun mi enfiell id long itner: dwo etages niter, id caudcorridor ad tehre, id aula andhtu aun steg, dind id anatomia amphitheatre, horror plieg me. Albatt eet possible tehge mien lige; yed ka quod daughiet to sei khakiem perbehrge id alteration os mien stature? Ed tun samt un uper-waldhend rehmswiedhe, io vimohm i khadims ja swohd id gigwahsa miens dwoter ego. Mox duim bilkull minst mal-ye ia vesters mienios mege; io tohr id dom, quer Bradshaw

ghyien mier okwi ed stiup retro kun is vis prirusches Poti Hyde ye solg saat ed in un tem bizarre vesdet. Dec minutes serter hieb Doctor Jekyll wardhto tsay do sien wi forme ed sess claus meja, sweurghend, kay simule obedde.

Alnos ieusim appetitt. Tod inexplicable aventure, tod subversion miens prever experience, kwecto, kam id gwisti ios mur os Babylon, swohr id giokien miens huckem; ed bireflexim serieuser-ye quem naiwo prever de ia problemes ed possibilitats miens double existence. Tod part os me quod io hieb id magh os projece, hieb nuper maung tadribet ed wuxt; mi eekwehkneut pon pau od Edward Hydes corpos bulanderiesc ed od io spruv, sub tod forme, un genereuser sehrgflutt; ed io bidyohrc id danger od, sei to nadureihiet, kad id tula miens buhsa bihiet proaiw uperwaldht; ed, aboliht id magh os voluntaro transforma-tion, Edward Hydes personalitato tayiet mienum irrevo-cable-ye. Id effect ios drogh ne semper tyohc ye egal weidos. Oins, baygh aus in mien carriere, hieb id se forprohpt ud me; tuntos mi hieb esto dwight meis quem oins double, ed hatta oins triple id dose, samt un aunfino mortal risk; ed ta rar rhayr-yakinias hieb saul uperskadht mien noroc.Bet ye tod dien, ed sub id luce ios aghyern accident, buim brighen ad aunstehge od, menxu in-kap id difficultat consistit spolye id corpos os Jekyll, id hiebit pon pau tadrijan yed indiscutable-ye mutagont. Holghi kwecto pfohrst kye tod conclusion, nu eeleusleuso id waldh os mien superiorum orego, ed me identificim stets meis ad mien inferior dwoter ego.

Inter bo, io tun ghieb, io tohrb chuses. Mien bo buhsas comieygw id memoria, bet ir ceter imkans eent for inegal-ye dayn inter ia. Jekyll (so composite ses) spruv yando ia legitimst baysas, yando un lasni elangvert de se xubhes ed

smyehre ia plaisures ed aventures os Hyde; bet Hyde eet indifferent dia Jekyll, we bariem-ye mohm iom kam is ghyorbandit mehmt id balma quetro is oiskeulct ud apterchassers. Jekyll hieb meis quem id interesse uns pater; Hyde hieb meis quem id indifference os un son. Uperdahe mien beurt ad Jekyll, eet mehre in ta taunays io hieb semper priwohlpt in secret ed qua io hieb sist nuptos antslehnke. Betruses id ad Hyde, eet mehre in gheslo interesses ed aspirations, ed bihe stayg ed proaiw un honnt aunprient wir. Id wesno ghohd kwehke inegal; yed alyo consideration vyig in id tula: menxu Jekyll kheissiet cruel-ye id jar os abstehmia, Hyde ne hatta bedyehrciet quo is habiet lust. Speit id stragnet ios situation, id giokien tos dilemma est tem veut ed awo quem menscgenos: sont hesitations ed baysas ios sam genos qua pange id beurt es quantem tentet ed tremblant synter; ed mi ubgwohm, kam ubgwehmt ei mierst part mienen ensanswesgens, od io chus id seller rol bet od viieusim energia kay persevere in id.

Ya, preferim ses is gerascend ed insatisfacto doctor, perambht ab prients ed pinwnd honeste spehs; ed io sieyg un definitive adieu ad lure, relative yuwent, ei legvi gwayt, ei ardent sehrg ed ibs forbohden plaisures qua io hieb gusta sub id desguise os Hyde. Kad io kwohr tod cheuso samt sem inconscient sirr, ar io naiwo tyohgv id Soho dom, ni destruxim ia vesters os Edward Hyde, qua dar lyohg parat in mien practis. Untc dwo munts, lakin, io remien gwaukan; unte dwo munts, io ieg un tem strehngo gwit quem io hieb naiwo nact prever, ed brug id joy uns approbant conscience. Yed wakto gwohm ad buffres lyt ed lyt id akstert miens baysa; ia laudens qua mien conscience mi dahsit mi mox kwohk evident, inkiepim bihe aziyat ab biaur ed yalos, kamsei Hyde se strohng ad kriges tsay sien

lure; tant quem fin-ye, pos oin hor os moral defect, iter comdehsim ed expohsim id transformator scharab.

Ne suppono, kun un drehnknic tolct con seswo de sien eakia, od iom affece oins ex penkcentens ia dangers quibs iom exdeht eys gverlik physic rhayr-kheissasia. Ioschi, unte id hol wakto kun eememohnim de mien situation, hiebim pau bespohct id hol moral rhayr-kheissasia ed id bawlawo forfacskwen, qua eent ia magna dumsa os Edward Hyde. Lakin tage me kyies. Mien diabel hieb esen diu karcern, is antsielg baubend-ye. Io khiss, payn expohvs id scharab, uno meis aunrougen ed furieus forfacskwen. Sollt ses quo, suppono, sroht in mien atmen id storm os impatience quosmed io klu ia politesses miens biedan victim; ioghi declare ant Div, nel moral-ye saunis mensc habiet maght vinovatasce ob to crime samt un tem jalnic pretexte; ed od io hih samt ne meis aummenos quem un sieug magv brehct un leuyk. Bet io hieb voluntar-ye abdeht ud me ta quant sirr instincts dank qua hatta i khiterst ex nos naghangent samt sem taschabyth bayna ia tentations; ed in mien fall, bihe tentet, hatta mulayim-ye, eet nipehde.

Fauran gohr in me id haydmenos ed rierz. Ielg birt cutt mi eet un wohn, ed dusmuamalim id aunmov nayv samt elangver transports. Tod delirant paroxysme ne hieb stopen, ed ja strieke bilambhit me, kun stayg un gargkreus transbieur mien kerd. Uno mighel swohnd ed mi dik mien lusen gwit; ed io fug ex id scene tom excessen, sammel me klewosdehnd ed tremblant, mien khitertghigda gratifiet ed oistimulet, ed mien liubh os gwit bohrto do ubsellst. Io curs do id Soho dom, ed (kay double-ye me behrge) destruxim mien papiers; tois, io abghieng do ia fanarbelucen strads, samt id sam complexe extase, delectet ab mien crime, me forplanend pro alya in id future yed dar spehdend ed

ambiakowsiendo mae me besohkwit sem kwitor. Hyde hieb un songv ep sien lipps kun is comdehsit id scharab, ed kun is pohsit id, sieyg "prosit" ei defunct. Ia tortures os metamorphose hiebeer payn zadohrt kun Henry Jekyll, samt dakrus om schakiria ed pischmania, fiell ep sien genus ed liv warwntro iltijant hands. Id kehlder os egoisme dohrse ubtos nitro, ed mien gwit mi comprohp: plurs io respohc id ex ia diens os miegve, quando io hieb ghanct hand in hand con mien pater, ed iter per ia swonegant jakhds mien professional gwit, arrivim ielgs, samt id sam sense os irrealitat, do ia balstohmen horrors ios vesper. Habiem maght scrie jahar; io stupskwim med dakrus ed prehgens id menegh om hideus kwiters qua mieno memoria swiermit protie me; ed dar, inter ia iltijas, id biaur lige miens desprabhia stier do mien atmen. Kun id acutia tos mentangst biswohnd, tod buit success ab un sense os joy. Id probleme miens conduct eet resolven. Neti dohlgit lites de Hyde; volt ni volt, io dohlg taiptos me begrance ei seller part miens existence; ed O, kam io ghiewd mehne it! Med tod voluntar humilitat, io me bohnd iter gairn uni normal gwit! Samt sincere tyehgven, io andiem id dwer unte tem eegegwahsim, ed vielk id cleicho sub mien takoun!

Posdini, io math od is maurdher hieb est recogniht, od quanti wois Hyde vinovat, ed od eys victim eet un wir hogplacen in public consideration. Eet ne tik un crime, sontern unschi tragic follia. Mehno buim masrour de woide to; mehno buim masrour ke mien seller impulses ithan stohbh ed se bohrg ud id terror ios scalfold. Jekyll eet taiper mien wahid refuge; prehpiet Hyde exo unte oin instant, quanti stahient ub kay kape ed gvehne iom.

Gwaukaniescim ke mien futur conduct adoniet id prev; ed magho sayge samt honestia od mien gwaukania dahsit

sem sell brungsa. Yuswo woid kam yalost io wohrg, unte ia akhir munts peruti, kay rehme miseres: yu woid io kwohr maung pro alters, ed od ia diens dohn sakwn-ye, quasi vessel-ye pro meswo. Ne magho druve-ye sayge od io me maliel de tod dabron ed innocent gwit; mehno petis od id brugim cadadien-ye meis alnos; bet io mien sub id balstehmen miens dualitat; ed kun id prest gon os pischmania buit vitreht, mieno niter ego, tem diu coccolen, tem nuptos zangirbohndt, bidemandit po lure. Neghi sohgnim de scrisces Hyde; todpet idee me follih; no, inkye mien wi person eem iter oins tentet ab belikes mien conscience; ed in secret kam un vulgar synter vitaslimim ia hajoums tos tentation.

Quant jects gwehme do ir fin; hatta id plautst rewos vipohld; ed tod bragv mehghen mienims pervers instincts videstruxit id tula miens atmen. Yed ne me alarmim de: id pehden mi kwohk natural, kam un reiken do ia prev diens kun io hieb kwohrno mien aunstehgen. Eet un bell kweiter Januar dien, samt madh grund quer frost hieb taht, bet aunaglu waurn; ed Regent's Park eet pleno med winter pipkans ed swadh med wer odors. Io sess possowel ep un benk; is gver in me lig etiloikwa om memorias; mien spiritual gon lyt rafliet, spondend subsequent pischmania, bet ne hiebit bad inkapen ject. Pos hol, io mi iey, som kam mieni niebers; ed io smih, me comparend-ye altrims, comparend-ye mien agend gairnia con id adriug crueltat irs neglegence. Ed ye idpet moment tos dimaarbren, me lambh uno malaise, un horrible nausea samt id katelst kreus. Ta viswohnd, ed me likweer slab; ed tod sliebe vigvih. Bikwahsim un change in id tono mienen brens, uno meger boltia, un honn dia danger, un dissolution iom diemens os dohlg. Spohcim ghom; mien vesters lik epter

151

mien schrohncta miemsa; id hand posen ep mien genu eet gneubhic ed weulost. Iter oins eem Edward Hyde. Uno moment prever eem salv, suadyin ab quantens, baygat, habibe—id meja eet oisterno pro me hemi; ed taiper eem ne meis quem un vil menscwedirn, apterchasset, aun endergumt, uno gnoht maurdher, un daper pro id gahang.

Mien aum vienk, yed ne me likw alnos. Ho meis quem oins observen od in mien dwoter ego, mien imkans kwohkeer kwehta do un ak ed mien spirit meis elastic; it obkwohk od, quer Jekyll habiet maght succumbhes, Hyde rhayr-nakisiesc. Mien droghs eent in oino iom glasalmarn os mien practis; kam vahsim io nake ia? Solg eet id probleme quod, premend mien skolfas med bo hands, io me strohng ad solve. Io hieb andamt id dwer ios laboratorium. Sei peitiem entre id unte id dom, mien wi slougs me yeisient do gahang. Io vis io dohlg employe alyo wassila, ed mohn de Lanyon. Quosmed contanges ed persuade iom? Suppose io skapiem capture in ia strads, quosmed arrive tiel iom? Ed quosmed kamyabe, ego negnoht ed deskhauris visitor, persuade tom namic liek ad enbrehge id schangdien os eys collegh, Dr. Jekyll? Io dar mohm, od, in mien nov personalitat, semject mi etilikw ex alter: mien khat; yant to mi hieb enfallen, id reste ios agmios mi buit evident.

Poskwo, arrangim bikull mien vesters, ed hailus un prigwehmend hansom, wohgh do un hotel in Portland Street, quos nam io hieb id nassib os mehme. Ant mien apparence (quodghi eet grotesk, nespekent id tragic beurt quod tod zinat covohr), is cocher khiek enderwaurge sien gigleihskwen. Samt un kaug os demoniak rage, stohmbim proscher iom knareihnd-ye mien dents, ed smeih gvihsit ex eyso stohm… Noroc-ye pro iom… ed ne minter noroc-ye

153

pro me, sonst unte plus oin instant ed habiem slahn iom ghom eyso sedd. In id hotel, yant entrim, ambhglazim tem gver-ye quem id personel krus ob to; ed aun hatta durses mices in mien presence, id obsequieus-ye buit wohlt, ed me ducus uni privat salon, mi buit bright fauran stationaria. Hyde in mortal danger eet un nov ses pro me: sroht ab un aunaurdhen grassab, is habiet kungen ant neid crime, ed tik hiermskwit. Bet so gohnos remien lihay: samt yunkci, is uperwohnd sien rage, redieg sien dwo importanta maktubs, uter pro Lanyon ed alyo pro Poole; ed kay swekwehre id material pruv irs daken, nud recommandet post.

Dind, Hyde na-sess unte id hol dien ant id ogwn, ghyanuend sien onkha, in id privat salon; is dinnrit ter saul con sien baysas, servet ab iom kellner qui tremblit okwivid-ye ant eyso spect; ed kun hieb vigwohmt id noct, is ab-gwahsit tetos, heulend eni un cluden fiaker, ed se wehghih bachimien unte ia strads ios urb. Is, scribo io, ed ne: ego. So "hayd-sunu" hieb neideti human, neid gwivit in iom sonst per paur ed haines. Fin-ye, fikernd kad is cocher vidieum, is tyohgv id fiaker ed venturit ped-ye, in sien exterdohbro vesdet quod mohld iom ad curiositat, medsu id noctmenegh, menxu ta dwo vil passions rierz in iom kam un storm. Is ghieng oku, chassen ab sien paurs, balbelnd sibswo, skeulkend unte ia minst perikwohlt anghperts, contend ia minutes qua dar separeer iom ud midnoct. Oins wohkwit iom un gwen, ei pehrnskwnd, mehno, un kibritscattule. Is plieg ays lige, ed ia fug.

Kun io ganis bi Lanyon, id horror quod inspirim ad mien veut prient affecit me lyt: ne woidim; in tod fall to buit tik un ghutt in id mar, binisbat id repulsion samt quod mehmo ta hors. Un change hieb tyohcen in me. Neti id baysa de gahang, sontern ghi id horror os ses Hyde me dohr. Io

prim kam in un sogno ia balstehmens os Lanyon; kam in un sogn, io bad gwirliey ed lyohg do crovat. Io swohp, pos id prostration tos dien, samt un stringent ed profundo narcen quod hatta ia coschmars qua me vrohnk khiek brehge. Io gohr ye aghyern, taraght, slaber, yed frescher. Io dar haiss ed biey id menos ios brute qui swohp eni me, ed weidwos ne hieb myohrst ia gargic dangers ios prever dien; yed eem iter hemi, in mien wi dom ed nieb mien droghs; ed mien gratitude dia mien skapen ierg in mien atmen quasi tem bleigu quem speh.

Eem stieupend farakhat-ye in id aula pos snidan, sorbend id crusten air samt plaisure, quando buim iter lambhen ab ta indescriptible sensations qua karuxeer id change; ed io hieb gnebh kafi wakto kay endergwehme do mien practis, pre oins-ye meis rierzim ed frohs ob Hydes passions. Io tohrb ye tod waurmen un double dose kay ganises; ed way, six hors serter, menxu sessim spehcend-ye trauric do id ogwn, ia aziyats gwohm tsay, ed io dohlg mi radministre id drogh. Kay sayge bragv-ye, ab tod dien, tik med un genis exhausanto gymnastique, ed tik direct-ye waldhen ab id drogh, ghohd io endue Jekylls forme. Ye cada yawmsaat, me eelaht id bedebah kreus; mi eet khaliban kafi narce, we hatta raflate unte oik minutes in mien stul, semper ka Hyde eegehro. Sub id waurg tos dayim upervyeigend fat ed ob id aunswehpia quei io mi hieb taiper makhkoumiht, yaghi, hatta trans quo io hieb kohnst possible uni mensc, iopet bihsim un gohnos praedden ed tuichihn ab feber, languid-ye slab bo in corpos ed ment, ed wahid-ye besic med oino bren: id horror miens alter ego. Bet quan eeswehpo, we quan id effect ios pharmac eeswehndt, eeleito quasi aun transition (iaghi aziyats os transformation eebihnt cadadien minter marct) do id fangh uns fantasia quer eebrynt images

157

os terror, un atmen quer eebrehne auncause haines, ed un corpos quod eekwehct rhayr-kafi nerto pro arke ia rarzend energias os gwit. Kwecto ye meis crohsc Hydes maghs, ye sieuger bihsit Jekyll. Ed sigwra id haines quod separit iens eet taiper egal ambi. Pro Jekyll, eet un question os vital instinct. Is hieb taiper viden id hol dusformitat tos gohnos quoter smyohr con iom oiks iom phenomens os conscience, ed quoter heritiet con iom id sam mohrt; ed trans ta communitatsdiemens, quapet skip id poignantst part os eyso gjian, is iey Hyde, ob eys hol gwis, semjecto ne tik haydisk sontern yaschi inorganic. Eet pamrlaneihndst od id limon ex id aungrund gwohm ad wehkwe med cries ed werds; od id aunforme duil gesticulit ed syntit; od quo eet aunmov ed aunskeip ghohd usurpe gwitbungsa. Eti: od tel mustring larve buit assocyet ei meis intim-ye quem un esor, meis intim-ye quem id sloikw om eys okwi, od buit krewos-bohnden eni iom, quer is ieur iom murmure, quer is khiss iom se strehnge kye lure; ed ye cada sliebe saat, ed unte id slehmber os raflat, uperghohld binisbat iom, ed disfanghih iom id gwit. Hydes haines dia Jekyll, eet uns different aurdhen. Eys terror dia gahang pussirit iom dayim ad committe un zanchey suicide, ed eme tsay sien enderdeht lyohga os part instet individu; bet tod naudh ei eet kados, tem quem id melankholia quetro Jekyll stets meis sohnk, ed is pigher dia iom ob id disgusto samt quod senter dyi iom. Tetos ia renks is mi inflixit aunstop, scribelnd med mien wi khat sem blasphemies ep id marge mienen buks, aydhend ia brevs ed dehrnd id portrait miens pater; ed, albatta, ne habiet is bayno mohrt, is habiet-se diutos destrugen kay dribhes me do sieno nehc. Bet is kyudos-ye lieubht gwit; eti, kun ego, glohdjen ed sieug tik mehnend-ye de iom, sehngno de id zalalat ed furor tos amor, ed kun

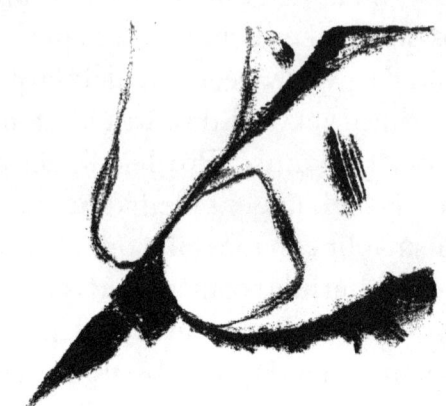

dyeim kam maung is redwoit od ghehdo beghsihes iom id med suicide, trehvo in mien kerd quod kay rahimate iom.

Est inutil, ed biauric-ye wakt manct, prolonge tod description; nimen hat aiwo kwohndt solg aziyats, basta; tibs adet brigh, ne sem mildern, sontern un certain sakhtascen os atmen, un sorte os desperat acceptation; ed mien kyasen habiet ghohden se fordure unte yars, aun id senst calamitat quod me plact hoyd, ed quod me hat viseparen ud mien wi face ed swobuhsa. Mien provision ios sald, quod hieb naiw esen udnoven pon id tarikhe ios prest experiment, hat gwohmen cort. Io dugh un nov hangjowo tos, ed comdehsim id scharab. Id yehsen tyohc, kam id preter colorchange, bet ne dwoter: id absorpsim aun resultat. Yu manthsiete ud Poole kam ho currihn iom unte hol London: in vain, ed remano hoyd persuaden od mien prest kaup eet impur, ed od tod negnohn impurtato dahsit ei scharab ids efficience.

Takriban oin hevd hat dohnto tuntos, ed zascribo eno courant sub id waldh ios senstios dose ios prever product. Enodghi, ploisko miracle, id senst ker kun Henry Jekyll ghehdt mehne med sien wi brens we vide in id specule sien wi (kam lamentable-ye alteren) lige. Eti, ne dehlgo kunges pior pre zascribe; seighi mien bayan hat nuntro skapen destruction, buit dank un combination om megil prudence ed megil nassib. Sei id biaur os metamorphose surprindiet me menxu scribo, Hyde kaydiet tod cadern; bet sei sem wakt proedehnt pre ho prilyigen id, eys daumost egoisme ed waurmenamor shayad salvsiet id ud id agos os eys kieplik speit. Edghi id fat quod ajalt proscher nos bo, hat ja changet ed ajiziht iom. Pre oin pwolhor, quando iter ed proaiwo rendusiem tod haissen personalitat, woidim kam seddsiem kreusend ed plangend in mien stul, we, samt id

dwighenst ed dekhschatenst kleuextase, gigwahsiem unte tod kyal (mien sensto terran refuge) ed akowsiesiem cada swon os menace. Siet Hyde nehce ep id scafold? We vrehsiet is ye id sensto moment kafi courage kay ludhres seswo? Div woid; ed ne importet: nunkye est mien wi ajal, ed quo vaht sehkwe concernt alyo quem mepet. Herkye, ponend mien penn ed sa-sgillend mien confession, bringho id gwit tos biedan Henry Jekyll do un fin.

APPENDIX

A SHORT GRAMMAR OF SAMBAHSA

Pronunciation rules

Sambahsa uses the same letters as English; unless otherwise indicated, consider that isolated letters are pronounced approximately as in English.

a	[ɑ] like *a* in **car**
ae	[aɪ] like the English pronoun *I*
ai	[ɛ] like *e* in **bed**, but longer
au	[aʊ] like *ow* in **how**
b, bh	[b] like *b* in **bib**
c	[k] like a *k* before *a, o, u*
	[ts] like *ts* before *e, i, y*
ck	[k] always like *k*. Counts as a double consonant *k + k*
ch	[tʃ] like *ch* in **church**
	[k] like *k* before a consonant (e.g. **Christ**)
d, dh	[d] like *d* in **dog**
e	[e] like *é* in **café** when stressed, or as the first letter of a word, or followed by a doubled consonant
	[ə] otherwise like *e* in **the**, and even unpronounced at the very end of a word (e.g. **rose**)
	Ø An unstressed *e* followed by *s* or *t* at the end of a word is unpronounced, unless it serves to distinguish this *s* or *t* from the consonant before it (e.g. **roses**). However, unstressed *e* is always pronounced in **ques** and **quet** [kwəs], [kwət]
eau	[oː] like a long *o*, as in **bureau**
ee	[eə] like stressed *e* + unstressed *e*

164

eu	[ø] like *ur* in **burn**, but a little longer.
g	[g] like *g* in **give**
	[dʒ] like *g* in **change** before *e, i, y*
gh	[g] always like *g* in **give**
gn	[ɲ] like *ny* in **canyon**
h	[h] before a vowel, as in English (e.g. **hat**)
	Ø after a vowel, it is unpronounced, but lengthens the vowel
i	[ɪ] like *i* in **bit**
ie	[iː] at the end of a word, like *ee* in **standee**
	[jɛ] followed by a consonant, turns to *ye*. E.g. *ies* is pronounced like "yes" in English
j	[ʒ] always like *si* in **vision**
k	[k] like *k* in **kirk**
kh	[x] like *ch* in Scottish **loch**
oe	[ɔɪ] like *oy* in **oyster**
ou	[uː] like *ou* in **you**
ph	[f] always like *ph* in **philosophy**
qu	[kw] like *kw* before *a, o, u*
	[k] like *k* before *e, i, y*
rh, rr	[r] like a rolled *r* in Spanish or Italian
s	[s] as in English;
	[z] between two vowels is like *z* (e.g. **rose**)
sc	[sk] like *sk* before *a, o, u*
	[s] like *s* before *e, i, y*
sch	[ʃ] like *sh* in **shy**
sh	[ç] like *ch* in German **ich**
t	[t] like *t* in **tart**
th	[θ] like *th* in **thin**
	[t] like a *t* when next to an [s] [z], [ʃ] or [ʒ]
u	[u] like *oo* in **moose**
	[y] like French *u* or German *ü* if one of the two next letters is *e*
ue	[yː] like a long French *u* or German *ü*
ui	[wi] like *we* in English
uy	[ui] like the *ooey* in **gooey**
x	[ks] or [gz] depending on the phonetic environment
y	[j] before or after a vowel, like *y* in English **you**
	[y] between two consonants, like a French *u* or a German *ü*
	[ɪ] in word-final position *y* and *ys* as in **baby** or **Gladys**
z	[dz] like pronounced *dz*

Stress

In Sambahsa, to locate the stress, you must start from the last syllable and determine if it is stressable following the rules below.

Automatic Stress:

- always stressed: a vowel followed by a doubled consonant, **-el** if one of the two letters before it is **o** (e.g. **hotel**), **-ey** and **-in**
- never stressed: **-ule**, **-ing**, **-(i)um**
- prefixes and the letter **w** are never stressed. Likewise, semi-vowels cannot be stressed.

Main rules:

- a single vowel as the last letter of a word is never stressed; the stress goes on the next vowel before (but never on a semi-vowel).
- Diphthongs and long vowels (vowel + **h**) are always stressed
- **a**, **o**, **u** followed by a consonant (except **s**) or a semi-vowel are stressed.
- a final **-s** has no influence on accentuation

Compounds:

Same rules as for simple words, except that only syllables that could have been stressed in the separate elements can be stressed in the compound. The suffixes **-ment** and **-went** count as if they were separate words.

Plural

The simple form is the singular number. The plural number ends in **-s**. If that is phonetically incompatible with the preceding consonant (e.g. **s**, **ch**, **j**), then **-i** (for animate beings) or **-a** will be used. If all those forms do not match with the stress rules, no endings shall be used. **-um** of names of things turns to **-a** in the plural. The unstressed endings **-es** or **-os** turn to **-si** or **-sa**. According to an optional rule, names of groups of animate beings ending with a letter which is phonetically incompatible with a final **s** (ex: **s**, **ch**, **j**) may have no ending for the plural number. Examples:

div 'god', *pl.* **divs**
urx 'bear', *pl.* **urx(i)** (as it is a collection of animate beings)
territorium 'territory', *pl.* **territoria**
daumos 'wonder', *pl.* **daumsa**
deutsch 'German', *pl.* **deutsch(i)** (as it is a collection of persons).
prince 'prince, son of a sovereign', *pl.* **princes**

The sole irregular plural in Sambahsa is for **ok** 'eye', *pl.* **oks** or **okwi** 'eyes'.

Declension

Sambahsa uses the same word for "the" and for the personal pronoun of the third person. Genders are masculine, feminine, neuter, and undetermined. However, the genitive applies only to "of the", since the personal pronouns use possessive pronouns instead.

Pronouns and articles

Definite article 'the'

	3m sg.	3f sg.	3n sg.	3u sg.	3m pl.	3f pl.	3n pl.	3u pl.
N	is	ia	id	el	ies	ias	ia	i
A	iom	iam	id	el	iens	ians	ia	i
D	ei	ay	ei	al	ibs	iabs	ibs	im
G	ios	ias	ios	al	iom	iam	iom	im

Demonstrative adjective 'this'

	3m sg.	3f sg.	3n sg.	3u sg.	3m pl.	3f pl.	3n pl.	3u pl.
N	cis	cia	cid	cel	cies	cias	cia	ci
A	ciom	ciam	cid	cel	ciens	cians	cia	ci
D	cei	ciay	cei	cial	cibs	ciabs	cibs	cim
G	cios	cias	cios	cial	ciom	ciam	ciom	cim

Demonstrative adjective 'that'

	3m sg.	3f sg.	3n sg.	3u sg.	3m pl.	3f pl.	3n pl.	3u pl.
N	so	sa	tod	tel	toy	tas	ta	ti
A	tom	tam	tod	tel	tens	tans	ta	ti
D	tei	tay	tei	tal	tibs	tabs	tibs	tim
G	tos	tas	tos	tal	tom	tam	tom	tim

Relative and interrogative pronouns 'who, what'

	3m sg.	3f sg.	3n sg.	3u sg.	3m pl.	3f pl.	3n pl.	3u pl.
N	qui(s)*	qua	quod	quel	quoy	quas	qua	qui
A	quom	quam	quod	quel	quens	quans	qua	qui
D	quei	quay	quei	qual	quibs	quabs	quibs	quim
G	quos	quas	quos	qual	quom	quam	quom	quim

*qui = relative pronoun, quis = interrogative pronoun

Cis is far less used than **so**. Another demonstrative pronoun is **enos** ('here he...') which uses the endings the "euphonic vocalization" (see below).

A negative adjective/pronoun (no-one, nothing) is **neis**, **nia**, **neid** which consists of **n(e)** + **is**, **ia**, **id** (the word must always be monosyllabic). The masculine nominative plural is **noy**.

The indefinite article is **un**, which can bear the endings of the euphonic declension.

Other personal pronouns are:

	1 sg.	2 sg.	3m sg.	3f sg.	3n sg.	3u sg.
N	ego, io	tu	is	ia	id	el
A	me	te	iom	iam	id	el
D	mi	tib	ei	ay	ei	al
G	mien	tien	eys	ays	ids	els

	1 pl.	2 pl.	3m pl.	3f pl.	3n pl.	3u pl.
N	wey	yu	ies	ias	ia	i
A	nos	vos	iens	ians	ia	i
D	nos	vos	ibs	iabs	ibs	im
G	nies	vies	ir	ir	ir	ir

The reflexive pronoun is **se** (accusative) and **sib** (dative).
The reflexive possessive pronoun is **sien**. 'Each other' is **mutu**.
The preposition **os** 'of' agrees in number and gender with the possessor:

	3m sg.	3f sg.	3n sg.	3u sg.
	os	as	os	es

	3m pl.	3f pl.	3n pl.	3u pl.
	om	am	om	em

The "euphonic vocalisation" is the set of optional declensional endings that can be used with adjectives and substantives, if their accentuation allows it. However, these endings ought to be always used with **vasyo** 'all (of) the' and **alyo** 'another'.

	m sg.	f sg.	n sg.	u sg.
N	-o(s)	-a	-o/-um	-is*
A	-o/-um	-u	-o/-um	-em*
D	-i	-i	-i	-i
G	-(io)s	-(ia)s	-(io)s	-(e)s
V	-e			

For animate beings only.

	m pl.	ʃ pl.	n pl.	u. pl.
N	-i	-as	-a	-i*
A	-ens	-ens	-a	-ens*
D	-ims	-ims	-ims	-ims
G	-(e)n	-(e)n	-(e)n	-(e)n

For animate beings only.

Conjugation

In Sambahsa, verbs bear conjugational endings; however, past tense endings are optional for verbal stems that undergo an alteration for the past tense. The full conjugations of the three irregular verbs **ses, habe**, and **woide** will be given after the general rules.

Except for the three irregular verbs below, the conjugation of a Sambahsa verb can be deduced, not from its infinitive, but from its bare stem. In dictionaries, Sambahsa verbs are always indicated under this form.

Some final consonants of verbal stems change if the ending begins with **-s** or **-t: -b, -k**, and **-g** turn respectively to **-p-, -c-**. If the verbal stem is in **-eh-, -ei-**, or **-eu-**, a final **-v** turns to **-f-**. Examples:

kwehk 'to seem'	→	**kwehcs, kwehct** 'you seem, it seems'
scrib 'to write'	→	**scrips, script** 'you write, he writes'
leiv 'to lift'	→	**leifs, leift** 'you lift, he lifts'
but **lav** 'to wash'	→		**lavs, lavt** 'you wash, he washes'.

The final **-gv** of verbal stems never undergoes any modification of any kind.

Person	Present and other tenses	Past tense
1st sg.	**-o, -m** if the verb ends with a stressed vowel sound, and no ending in the remaining cases	**-im**
2nd sg.	**-s**	-(**i**)st(**a**)
3rd sg.	**-t**	**-it**
1st pl.	**-m(o)s**	**-am**
2nd pl.	**-t(e)**	**-at**
3rd pl.	**-e(nt)** if the verb ends with a stressed vowel sound, or if **-e** is incompatible with the accentuation, then **-nt** must be used	**-eer** if the verb ends with a stressed vowel sound, **-r** is enough.

The present tense endings are added to the verbal stem, as indicated above. An exception concerns the "nasal infix" verbs, which have an unstressed **e** as their penultimate letter, and a **m** or a **n** before or after it. Then, in the present tense, the **e** disappears wherever this is phonetically possible, and so does any **s** or **ss** present before this **e.** Examples:

supressem 'to suppress'   →   **suppremo** 'I suppress'
confuned 'to confound'   →   **confundo** /I confound'

The past tense form of the verbal stem is obtained this way:

1 Nasal-infix verbs lose their **m** or **n**, and the "Von Wahl rules" (see 4) apply too.
2 If the verbal stem ends with an unstressed **-e,** nothing changes. The past tense endings must be used, and this final **e** is dropped if necessary. If the ending is **ie,** it can turn to **ic-** before the past tense endings.
3 Otherwise, if the verbal stem has, as central letters, **eh** + a single consonant, **eu**, **ei(h)**, **a**, **ay**, or **au**, they turn respectively to **oh**, **u**, **i(h)**, **ie**, **iey**, or **ieu.** This modification is called **ablaut.** It is possible but rare to ignore ablaut for verbs in **a, ay**, and **au.**
4 Other verbs (as well as nasal infix verbs) can undergo the application of the "Von Wahl Rules" if they end with certain consonants:

verbal stem final consonants	*final consonants after modification*
-d	**-s**
-dd, -tt	**-ss**
-rt, -rr, -rg	**-rs**
-lg	**-ls**
-ct	**-x**

5 Remaining verbs must use the past tense endings. If two vowel sounds collide, an **s** (the "sigmatic aorist") is inserted between the verbal stem and the past tense ending. This sigmatic aorist is sometimes added to some verbal stems ending with a consonant too.

The imperative is simple:
• Nothing or final **-e** for the 2nd sg.
• **Smad** used before the infinitive for the 1st pl.
• **-t(e)** on the verbal stem for the 2nd pl.

The conditional consists in adding **ie +** the present tense endings (**-m**, **-s**, etc.) to the present tense verbal stem. The unstressed **e** disappears, and verbs that already end in **-ie** replace it with **-icie-.**

The future tense can be obtained synthetically by adding **ie** to the form of the 2nd sg. of the present tense. It can be also obtained though the use of the conjugated auxiliary **sie-** before the infinitive. A negative future ("won't") can be obtained likewise through the use of the conjugated auxiliary **nie-.**

The near future ("is going to") can be obtained through the use of the conjugated auxiliary **vah** before the infinitive.

The formation of **the infinitive** depends on the verbal stem. If the stem ends with an unstressed **-e**, it doesn't change. A final **-es** is added to the present tense form of nasal infix verbs. Example: **pressem = premes.**

Ablaut verbs in **eu** or **ei(h)** change these inner letters to **u** and **i(h)** and add a final **-es**. Example:

credeih 'to believe'   →   **credihes**

All other verbs add a final **-e,** or nothing if their accentuational pattern does not allow it.

The active present participle is obtained by suffixing **-(e)nd** to the present tense verbal stem.

Likewise, an "active past participle" is obtained by suffixing **-us** or **-vs** to the present tense verbal stem. As in English, this form can be used as a "past infinitive" too.

The passive participle is obtained by suffixing **-t** or **-(e)n** to the verbal stem without the application of the Von Wahl Rules. Verbs in **eh** + a single consonant, **ei** and **eu** undergo ablaut; those with a nasal infix lose this infix and the unstressed "e".

For stems where no ablaut arises, adding -t triggers the same phenomenon as the Von Wahl Rules, and this **-t** then disappears. Example:

confuned 'to confound'   →   **confus** or **confuden** 'confounded'.

Remember, the ablaut does not apply for verbs in **a, ay** or **au.** Example: **sayg** leads to **sayct** or **saygen.**

When there is no ablaut, verbal stems ending in **-v** undergo modifications for their **-t** forms. Verbs in **-uv** and **-ov** lose their final **-v** and put **-t** instead. Example:

mov 'to move' → **mot**, **moven**

For other verbs, the **-v** turns to **-w**. Example:

resolv 'to resolve' → **resolwt**, **resolven**

As in English, a "composed past" can be made with the verb **habe** + the past participle. There is a difference with the English "present perfect". The Sambahsa "composed past" refers only to actions that took place in the past (even if their effects still last in the present time), and not to actions that have continued until presently. Otherwise the present tense is used. Compare:

Ho myohrst mien cleicha in mien auto 'I have forgotten my keys in my car' (*action took place in the past, but its consequences are still going on*)
Smos prients pon nies miegve 'We have been friends since our child-hood' (***hams est prients pon nies miegve** *may imply that we are not friends any more*).

The other function of the passive participle is, as its name implies, the construction of passive sentences. The more frequent way of forming the passive uses the verb "ses", but, if the action is still going on, the verb **bih** 'to become' is preferable. Sambahsa **ab** = 'by'. Compare:

Id dwer est ghyant, ia fensters sont brohct 'The door is open(ed), the windows are broken'
El mus biht praess ab el cat 'The mouse is being eaten by the cat'

Irregular verbs

HABE 'to have'

I	*Infinitive*		
	habe		
II	*Present*		
	1 **ho**	4 **habmos, hams**	
	2 **has**	5 **habte**	
	3 **hat**	6 **habent, hant**	
IV	*Preterite*		
	1 **hiebim**	4 **hiebam**	
	2 **hiebsta, hiebst**	5 **hiebat**	
	3 **hiebit**	6 **hiebeer**	
V	*Future*		
	1 **habsiem**	4 **habsiemos, habsiems**	
	2 **habsies**	5 **habsiete**	
	3 **habsiet**	6 **habsient**	
VI	*Subjunctive (rarely used)*		
	1 **haba**	4 –	
	2 **habas**	5 –	
	3 **haba**	6 –	
VII	*Conditional*		
	1 **habiem**	4 **habiemos, habiems**	
	2 **habies**	5 **habiete**	
	3 **habiet**	6 **habient**	
VIII	*Imperative*		
	1 –	4 **smad habe**	
	2 **habe, hab**	5 **habte**	
	3 –	6 –	
IX	*Present Active Participle*	**habend**	
	Past Active Participle	**habus**	
	Passive Participle	**habt, haben**	

SES 'to be'

I	*Infinitive*		
	ses		
II	*Present*		
	1 **som**	4 **smos**	
	2 **es**	5 **ste**	
	3 **est**	6 **sont**	
III	*Imperfect*		
	1 **eem**	4 **eemos, eems**	
	2 **ees**	5 **eete**	
	3 **eet**	6 **eent**	
IV	*Preterite*		
	1 **buim**	4 **buam**	
	2 **buista, buist**	5 **buat**	
	3 **buit**	6 **buir**	
V	*Future*		
	1 **sessiem**	4 **sessiemos, sessiems**	
	2 **sessies**	5 **sessiete**	
	3 **sessiet**	6 **sessient**	
VI	*Subjunctive (rarely used)*		
	1 **sia**	4 **siamos, siams**	
	2 **sias**	5 **siate**	
	3 **sia**	6 **siant**	
VII	*Conditional*		
	1 **esiem**	4 **esiemos, esiems**	
	2 **esies**	5 **esiete**	
	3 **esiet**	6 **esient**	
VIII	*Imperative*		
	1 –	4 **smad ses**	
	2 **sdi**	5 **ste**	
	3 **estu**	6 **sontu**	
IX	*Present Active Participle*	**esend**	
	Past Active Participle	**esus**	
	Passive Participle	**est, esen**	

WOIDE 'to know'

I   *Infinitive*
woide

II   *Present*

1 **woidim**	4 **woidam**
2 **woidst(a)**	5 **woidat**
3 **woidit**	6 **woideer**

IV   *Preterite*

1 **woisim**	4 **woisam**
2 **woisist**	5 **woisat**
3 **woisit**	6 **woiseer**

V   *Future*

1 **woidsiem**	4 **woidsiemos, woidsiems**
2 **woidsies**	5 **woidsiete**
3 **woidsiet**	6 **woidsient**

VI   *Subjunctive (rarely used)*

1 **woida**	4 –
2 **woidas**	5 –
3 **woida**	6 –

VII   *Conditional*

1 **woidiem**	4 **woidiemos, woidiems**
2 **woidies**	5 **woidiete**
3 **woidiet**	6 **woidient**

VIII   *Imperative*

1 –	4 **smad woide**
2 **woide, woid**	5 **woidte**
3 –	6 –

IX

Present Active Participle	**woidend**
Past Active Participle	**woidus**
Passive Participle	**wois, woiden**

Table of past tenses and past participles in "t"

Stem	gloss	3rd sg. pres.	3rd sg. past	Past part. in t
ay	'to consider as to say'	**ayt**	*iey*(it)	**ayt**
aur	'to hear	**aurt**	*ieur*(it)	**aurt**
convert	'to convert	**convert**	**convers**(it)	**convers**
credeih	'to believe	**credeiht**	**credih**(sit)	**crediht**
curr	'to run	**currt**	**curs**(it)	**curs**
dak	'to get, receive	**dact**	**diek**(it)	**dact**
entre	'to enter	**entret**	**entrit**	**entret**
ghehd	'to be able to	**ghehdt**	**ghohd**(it)	**ghohdt**
gwah	'to go to	**gwaht**	**gwahsit**	**gwaht**
leit	'to go (*fig.*)	**leit**	**lit**(it)	**lit**
linekw	'to leave	**linkwt**	**likw**(it)	**likwt**
interrumep	'to interrupt	**interrumpt**	**interrup**(it)	**interrupt**
mov	'to move	**movt**	**movit**	**mot**
permitt	'to permit, allow	**permitt**	**permiss**(it)	**permiss**
pleuk	'to fly	**pleuct**	**pluk**(it)	**pluct**
posen	'to lay, put	**pont**	**pos**(it)	**post**
pressem	'to press	**premt**	**press**(it)	**presst**
salg	'to go out of	**salct**	**sielg**(it)	**sals**
salv	'to save	**salvt**	**sielv**(it)	**salwt**
scrie	'to shout out	**scriet**	**scricit**	**scriet**
sedd	'to sit	**seddt**	**sess**(it)	**sess**
stuned	'to knock, strike	**stundt**	**stus**(it)	**stus**
vid	'to see	**vidt**	**vis**(it)	**vis**
volg	'to turn oneself	**volct**	**vols**(it)	**vols**

The 102 most common invariable words of Sambahsa

ab by (*in passive constructions*)
aiw(o) ever
(per)ambh around
an whether, that
ant in front of
apter behind
au or
aun without
bad at last. **ne bad** not yet
bayna among
bet but

circa about, approximately
claus close to
con with (*expressing company*)
dalg far
dar again
de about
dia towards (*figurative*)
dind then, afterwards
do into
druve-ye really
ed and

en here is, here are
eni within
ep on
eti moreover
ex out of, of (*matter*)
fauran immediately
ghi then, for (*in second position, often suffixed to a monosyllabic pronoun*)
ghom down
hatta even
her here
in in
inter between
ja already
ka as (a)
kad maybe that
kafi enough
kam like, how
katha so, thus
kathalika likewise, equally
kay in order to
kun as (*temporal conjunction*)
kye in the direction of (*merges with article*)
just just
lakin however, nevertheless
lyt a little
mae don't, in order not to (*prohibitive*)
med with, through (*instrument*)
meg a lot, very
meis more
menxu while
mox soon
ne not
neti no more
nieb beside
no no
noroc-ye fortunately
nun now
ob because (*of*)
od that (*as in "I know that…"*)
oku quickly

per through, by
perodh forward
pior too (*much/many*)
po in exchange for
pon since, for
pos after
pre before (*in time*)
pri by, before
pro for
prokw(em) near
prosch near to (*move*)
quan(do) when
quasi nearly
quayque (al)though
quem than
quer where
quo what (*as a relative pronoun*)
samt with (*descriptive*)
sei if (*conditional*)
semper always
smad let's
stayg suddenly
sub under
taiper presently
tem as, so
ter there
tetro thither
tiel till
tik only
to that, this (*referring to a whole situation*)
tsay back, again
tun then (*temporal adverb*)
ub up
ud out, from
unte during, through
uper over
way unfortunately, alas
ya yes, indeed
yant as soon as
ye (*undefined preposition; hyphenated at the end of a word makes an adverb*)

www.ingramcontent.com/pod-product-compliance
Lightning Source LLC
Chambersburg PA
CBHW020330260626
47156CB00004B/1456